THE CATTLEMAN'S
SPECIAL DELIVERY

THE CATTLEMAN'S SPECIAL DELIVERY

BY

BARBARA HANNAY

MILLS
BOON®

First published in Great Britain 2012
by Mills & Boon, an imprint of Harlequin (UK) Limited.
Large Print edition 2013
Harlequin (UK) Limited, Eton House,
18-24 Paradise Road, Richmond, Surrey TW9 1SR

© Barbara Hannay 2012

ISBN: 978 0 263 23181 6

CHAPTER ONE

JESS squirmed in the passenger seat as the car sped along the lonely outback road, windscreen wipers thrashing madly. At thirty-seven weeks pregnant, she would have found this journey tedious under any circumstances.

Tonight, in the inky, rain-filled darkness, with the wrong music playing and the monotonously annoying *swish*, *swish* of the wipers, the journey was definitely too late and too long and *far* too uncomfortable.

Beside Jess, her husband contentedly chewed gum and tapped the steering wheel, matching his rhythm to the latest hit from his favourite band. Alan was pleased with himself. Today he'd landed a new job managing an outback pub—a chance, at last, to earn regular wages. Jess had to admit she was pleased about this fresh start, away from the city temptations that had caused them so much trouble.

This morning, they'd travelled out to Gidgee Springs to view the pub and to settle the agreement, and in a few months, when their baby was old enough, Jess would probably work in the kitchen, so they'd both be earning again. Fabulous.

Admittedly, life in a tiny outback town wasn't quite what Jess had envisaged when she'd made her wedding vows, but she'd been pretty naïve the day she'd married Alan Cassidy on a romantic tropical beach at sunset. Now, three years older and wiser, she saw this new job as a much-needed chance to start over, to get things right. Finally.

As the car sped on Jess peered ahead, worried that the headlights seemed too feeble to fight with the rain. They barely picked up the white dividing lines on the narrow road and she was grateful that the traffic in the lonely outback was so sparse.

She closed her eyes, hoping she might nod off, found herself, instead, remembering the terrible day she'd almost walked out on Alan after he lost the last of their money on yet another hopeless business scheme. Jess had made the tough decision even though she'd known firsthand that single-motherhood was a truly difficult option.

She'd never known her own father, instead had grown up with her mother and serial 'uncles', and it wasn't the life she wanted. But she'd realised she had to leave Alan even though it would mean the death of her dreams of a proper, two-parent family. Those dreams had already crumbled to dust on the day Alan lost their entire savings.

Single, she would at least regain control over her income, and she would have found a way to keep a roof over her baby's head. Then, at the last minute, Alan had seen an ad for this job as manager of a pub. It was another chance. And Jess had stayed.

Years ago, her mother had warned that marriage was a gamble, that very, very few lucky souls could ever hope for a happy ending. Now Jess was taking one last gamble, praying that after today things would be different.

Surely they should be different.

Oh, please, let him be different.

They would finish this interminable drive back to Cairns. Their baby would be born in a few weeks' time and then the three of them would start their new life in Gidgee Springs.

She would give her marriage one last chance.

Reece Weston almost missed seeing the car in the ditch. He was about to turn into his cattle property when the headlights picked up the rounded hump of a dead kangaroo lying in the rain at the edge of the bitumen, and then skid marks veering off the road. Driving closer, he caught the gleam of white metal.

Dread settled uncomfortably in his gut as he pulled over. A small sedan had plunged nose-down into a rocky gully.

He knew the vehicle hadn't been there an hour or two earlier, and chances were he was the first person to come across it. Grim-faced, he grabbed a torch from the glovebox and slipped his satellite phone into his coat pocket.

The night was moonless and black and wind

threw rain into his face as he negotiated the slippery bank. The car's front passenger door hung open, the seat empty. Flashing the torch over the sides and bottom of the gully, Reece hoped he wasn't about to find a body flung from the crash. He couldn't see anyone outside the car, but when he edged closer to the wreckage he found the figure of a man slumped over the steering wheel.

Scrambling around the vehicle, he dragged the driver's door open, released the seat belt and felt for a pulse in the man's neck.

No luck.

He tried the wrist. Still no sign of life.

Sickened, he wrenched open the back passenger door, shoved a suitcase from the back seat into the rain, leaned in and lowered the driver's seat backwards into a reclining position. It would be hours before help could arrive, so saving this guy was up to him. Struggling to get beside the body in the cramped space, he began to apply CPR.

Come on, mate, let's get this heart of yours firing.

Reece had only done this on dummies before,

so he was by no means experienced, but he was glad the training came back to him now as he repeated the cycle over and over—fifteen compressions and two slow breaths.

He wasn't sure how long he worked before he heard the woman's cry coming from some distance away. The thin sound floated faintly through the rain, and for a split second he thought that perhaps he'd imagined the sound, a trick of the wind. But then he heard it again. Louder.

'Help, someone, please!'

Definitely a woman. She had to be the passenger, surely.

He grabbed his sat phone and punched in numbers for the district's one and only cop, praying there'd be an answer. To his relief the response was instant and he'd never been more pleased to hear the sergeant's gravel-rough voice.

'Mick, Reece Weston here. There's been an accident out near the turn off to my place—Warringa. A small sedan's hit a kangaroo and gone off the road. I've been trying CPR on the driver, but I'm not having much luck, I'm afraid. No signs of life. And now there's someone else calling for help. I'm going to check it out.'

'OK, Reece. I'll alert the ambulance at Dirranbilla, and come straight out. But you know it'll take me a couple of hours. And the ambos could be even longer. Actually, with all this rain, they might have trouble getting through. The creeks are rising.'

Reece let out a soft curse as he disconnected. Times like this, he had to ask why his forebears had settled in one of the remotest parts of Australia. He flashed his torch up and down the gully again, then scrambled onto the road and cupped his hands to his mouth. 'Where are you?' he called.

'On a track off the road. *Please...help!*'

The only track around here led into his homestead. The woman must have scrambled from the car in a bid to reach help for the driver. She sounded both scared and in pain.

Rain needled his face as he started to run, the beam of his torch bouncing ahead down the track, lighting muddy puddles and drenched grass and the slim trunks of gum trees. Rounding a bend, he found the woman huddled in the rain, sagged against a timber fencepost.

He flashed the torch over her and caught her pale, frightened face in its beam. Her hair was long and hanging in wet strings to her shoulders. Her arms were slender and as pale as her face, and she was holding something...

A step or two closer, he realised she was supporting the huge bulge of her heavily pregnant belly.

He was shocked to a standstill.

The man arrived just as the pain came again, huge and cruel, gripping Jess with a vice-like force. She tried to breathe with it, the way she'd been taught at antenatal classes, but no amount of breathing could bring her relief. She was too horrified and too scared. She wasn't supposed to be in labour now. Not three weeks early, not on the edge of a bush track in the rain and in the middle of nowhere. Not with Alan scarily unconscious and unable to help her.

The man stepped closer. She couldn't see him very well, but he seemed to be tall and dark-haired. Not old.

'Are you hurt?'

She shook her head, but had to wait till the contraction eased before she could answer. 'I don't think so,' she said at last. 'But I'm afraid my labour's started.'

He made a despairing sound. No doubt he wondered what the hell she was doing out here in an advanced state of pregnancy. She felt obliged to justify her predicament. 'My husband needs help. I was trying to find a homestead.'

By now his hand was at her elbow supporting her. Despite the rain, his skin was warm and she could feel the roughness of his work-toughened palm. She sensed she could trust him. She had no choice really.

'Alan's unconscious,' she said. 'I couldn't revive him, and then the pains started when I had to climb up the rocks to the road.' She gave a dazed shake of her head. 'I couldn't use my mobile. There's no network. But he needs an ambulance.'

'I saw him,' her rescuer said gently. He had brown eyes, as dark as black coffee, and he was watching her now with a worried frown. 'I've rung the local police and help is on the way. But, for the moment, I think you need to look after yourself and your little one.'

Jess's response was swallowed by a gasp as another contraction gripped her, then consumed her, driving every other thought from her head.

'Here, lean on me.' The stranger slipped his arm around her shoulders, steadying her against his solid chest.

Just having him there seemed to help.

'Thanks,' she said shyly when the pain was over.

'Look, you can't stay here.' Her good Samaritan slipped off his canvas coat and put it around her shoulders. 'This will at least keep the rain off you until I get you into the truck.' His voice was deep and kind. 'Can you wait here while I fetch it? I'll be as quick as I can.'

'Yes, of course.' She remembered to add, 'Thank you.'

He was gone then, but he was as good as his

word, and in no time the truck's headlights lit up the track. The door creaked a little as he opened it and swung down, his long legs seeming to stretch for ever. Before Jess knew quite what was happening, he'd scooped her up into his arms.

At first she was too overawed by his strength to protest, but she quickly came to her senses. 'For heaven's sake. I'm the size of a whale. I'll break your back.'

'Don't fuss. I'm not letting you climb up into this truck. There you go.' With a grunt he deposited her carefully on the front seat. 'We won't worry about the seat belt. I'll be careful and it's not far.'

'But we're not leaving, are we? What about Alan?'

'The ambulance and the police are on their way.' His voice was quiet, but commanding.

Jess gaped at him. Was he suggesting she should just abandon her husband? 'We can't leave him,' she protested. 'The poor man's unconscious. He's all alone.'

She began to tremble as she remembered how still and pale Alan had looked.

Watching her, Reece drew a sharp breath. Her eyes filled with tears and he had to turn away as he wrestled with this new dilemma. It would be too cruel to tell her bluntly that her husband was beyond help. Somehow, he had to keep her focused on her own needs.

'Seems you're about to have a baby,' he said as gently as he could. 'I'm guessing you wouldn't want to have it in a dirty truck's cabin.'

'Well…no.'

'I can give you a bed at the homestead. It's not much of a choice, I know, but, under the circumstances, I'm sure it's what your husband would want for you.'

Jess felt too confused and uncomfortable to argue. Now, sitting upright in the truck, she could feel her baby's head pushing down.

She felt terrible about leaving Alan, but she guessed she didn't really have a choice. Her priority now was their baby's safety, and almost as soon as the truck started up another contraction began. She dragged in a deep breath as the pain cut harder, deeper, lower, and she began to pant, staring out into the dark, rainy night, trying frantically not to moan and to concentrate instead on her breathing and the skinny trunks of gum trees flashing past.

No one had warned her that the pain would get this bad.

When it finally eased, her rescuer asked, 'Is this your first baby?'

Jess nodded. ''Fraid so. What about you? Has your wife been through this?'

'I don't have a wife,' he said quietly.

'Is there a woman at the homestead?'

'Unfortunately, no.'

Somehow, she managed to suppress a groan of disappointment. She'd been hoping to find a woman who'd been through this. Someone who could, at the very least, reassure her.

'By the way, my name's Reece.' He flashed a shy smile and for a moment his rather stern face looked incredibly appealing. 'Reece Weston.'

'Jess Cassidy. And I should have said—I'm so grateful to you.'

He shrugged. 'I'm glad I found you.'

'So am I, believe me.' She wondered if she ever would have made it, stumbling down this long, rough track in the rain on her own.

'Do you know if the baby's a boy or a girl?'

She supposed Reece was trying to take her mind off Alan.

'No,' she confessed. 'I didn't ask. I told the doctors I didn't want to know. I wanted a surprise.'

The sad truth was, she hadn't wanted Alan to know. He would have been so cocky and possessive if the baby was a boy, and at the time she'd still been undecided about whether she should stay with him.

And now… Oh, God, she felt another stab of guilt as she remembered how terribly pale and still Alan had been.

Was there a chance she'd panicked and overreacted? Maybe he was going to be OK. She was feeling so dazed, so sideswiped by the sudden onset of pain coming right on top of the accident.

Ahead of her now, through the rain, she could see a homestead at last. It was a typically North Queensland, timber dwelling, and ever so welcoming tonight with the golden glow of lights on the veranda. As they drew up at the front steps she saw two striped canvas squatter's chairs and a row of pegs holding battered Akubras and coats.

A stooped, elderly man appeared, squinting out at them like a short-sighted, bow-legged gnome.

In a blink, Reece was out of the truck and at Jess's door.

'I'm OK, thanks. Really, you don't have to lift me down.'

Once again he ignored her. 'Don't want you falling. I've got you.' He lifted her easily, and set her down lightly.

'Who you got there, son?'

'There's been an accident,' Reece told the old man. 'And this young lady needs to lie down. I'm going to put her in my room.'

'One of your fancy tarts, is she?'

Reece ignored this. 'Can you bring us some towels, Dad?' he asked instead.

With a strong arm around Jess, he steered her up a short flight of steps, and across the wooden veranda boards, not to the main front doorway, but to white-framed French doors. The rain hammered on the tin roof as Reece opened the doors and flicked on a light to reveal a large bed with an old-fashioned, blue chenille spread.

'Lean against the bedpost if you need to,' he said. 'I'll get rid of this bedspread.'

'You don't—' Jess's words were cut off as yet another contraction arrived.

Surely they weren't supposed to be so close together? She had no choice but to hang on to the bedpost and cope as best she could.

By the time the pain had eased, Reece had lit bedside lamps and turned the main light off, as well as pulling back the bedcovers. Now he was at her side, ready to help her out of the coat, just as his father arrived in the doorway, bearing towels.

The old man stared at her belly.

'This is Jess Cassidy, Dad.'

'Did you get her into trouble?'

Jess admired Reece's self-restraint as he simply

shook his head and said, 'I told you. There was an accident out on the main road.'

'Looks like she's about to drop.'

'Yes, Jess is in labour,' Reece said firmly as he took the towels. 'It would be helpful if you could fetch the Flying Doctors' medical chest. It's at the back of the pantry.'

The old man seemed reluctant to leave, but his son made a shooing gesture and, finally, he hobbled away.

Reece turned to Jess. 'You need to get out of these wet clothes.'

She was wearing a loose top over maternity trousers and, yes, they were wet, but the rest of her clothes were in a suitcase in the back of the car. 'I don't have anything else to change into.'

'You can wear one of my shirts.' Already he was opening a wardrobe, slipping a pale blue cotton shirt from a hanger. It looked almost big enough to serve as a nightgown.

His dark eyes were warm as he held it out to her. 'Can you manage?'

'Yes, thanks.' She would have to manage. She

certainly didn't want a handsome stranger helping her to undress, thank you very much. She knew very well that it would be a bachelor's worst nightmare to help a strange woman in an advanced state of pregnancy out of her clothes.

'I'll be fine,' she said to make sure he understood. But the words were no sooner out than she felt as if the bottom half of her were being wrenched away from her with massive force. She only just had time to grab to the bedpost before her knees gave way.

'Oh, God!' Seized by an overwhelming urge to bear down, she slumped against the post and clung for dear life. 'I'm so sorry,' she moaned. 'I think the baby's coming!'

And then her waters broke.

CHAPTER TWO

THE baby couldn't be coming already.

Reece stared at Jess in dismay. If she'd looked scared before, she now looked terrified, and he couldn't blame her. He was terrified too. This was way outside his experience. Weren't first babies supposed to take hours and hours to arrive?

He'd been confident that his job was to keep Jess comfortable until the Flying Doctor or the ambulance arrived—assuming that at least one of them could make it in this weather.

The poor girl.

Reece remembered her husband slumped over the steering wheel. If ever Jess Cassidy had needed her husband's support it was now.

'How can I stop this?' she moaned.

You can't, he wanted to tell her, and he wished he weren't so clueless. He'd only delivered calves—

mostly with a rope tied around the calf's hoof and his boot planted squarely on the mother's hind-quarter to gain leverage. That sure as hell wasn't going to work here.

'Maybe, if you lie down there'll be less pressure,' he suggested.

'That makes sense. I'll try anything.'

In this light, she looked little more than a girl, with her slender, pale limbs and long, dark hair hanging in limp, damp strands. Her thickly lashed eyes were green or grey—he couldn't be sure of their exact colour—and her nose was fine and slim, in contrast with the pink roundness of her soft mouth. In her wet, bedraggled clothes, she looked frail and helpless.

A wayside waif. In desperate need of his help.

He'd never felt more inadequate.

'You'll have to get out of these wet clothes,' he suggested.

This time Jess seemed ready to submit to his assistance and Reece held his breath as he helped her out of her shirt. It wasn't the first time he'd undressed a woman, although most of the women in his experience were very adept at slipping out of their gear.

This time was *so very* different, and he had to perform the delicate task with the dispassionate detachment of a medical practitioner.

Not so easy when Jess's skin was moon pale and smooth as sifted flour and when her body was lush and ripe with the fullness of her pregnancy. She was lovely. Earthy. Madonna-like. With an unexpected fragile beauty that could catch a man totally unprepared.

He was aware of her distress, however, and he worked quickly as, between them, they eased her maternity slacks down. He rubbed her back and legs dry with a fresh towel while she took care of her front. Then he squeezed moisture from her hair and rubbed at it with the towel.

Her bra was wet too, and he undid it gently, conscious that her full, round breasts might be tender.

When he helped her into his shirt, it came down almost to her knees and he had to roll the sleeves back several times to free her wrists. She kept her eyes downcast, no doubt embarrassed.

'Let's get you comfortable,' he said, helping her onto the bed.

His bed.

According to his mother, whom he hadn't seen in a decade, he'd been born in this room, although his younger brother, Tony, had been delivered in a hospital in Cairns, many hours' drive away.

Now, Jess lay on her side, an expression of fixed concentration on her face, her hand gently massaging her tense abdomen.

'I'm going to ring the Flying Doctor,' he said.

If they couldn't land in this rain, they could at least give him medical advice. He'd take all the advice he could get. This was his worst fear—a dependent woman on his isolated property, with no help for miles. His mother had been right. This was no place for women.

'Can I get you something from the kitchen, Jess? Would you like water?'

She gave a faint nod. 'Maybe a sip.'

He went quickly to the kitchen where he found his father cursing as he fiddled with the knobs on the radio.

'Can't get this damn thing to work.'

Reece sighed. 'Did you find the medical chest?'

His dad looked churlish. 'Forgot.'

'Can you get it now?' Reece gave another despairing sigh. This was a new problem that had arrived just lately—these signs that his father's short-term memory was deteriorating, along with his temper. But tonight he didn't have time to worry about it. 'I'm going to make some calls.'

His dad's face broke into a rare grin. 'At least I remembered to put the kettle on. You'll need boiling water, won't you?'

When Reece came back into the room with a medical chest, extra towels and a glass of water, Jess was fighting another urge to push, blowing frantically as she'd been taught in antenatal classes.

She heard the clink of the glass as Reece set it down on a bedside table.

'How are you doing?' he asked as the contraction finally loosened its grip.

'Awful,' she grunted. 'I'll tell you one thing. I'm never, *ever* having sex again.'

She saw him swallow a smile and she sent him a hefty scowl. It was all very well for guys. They got it easy—a night of fun and, nine months later, someone else endured giving birth to their child.

Perhaps it was just as well Alan wasn't here right now. She'd have given him a piece of her mind.

Oh, dear Lord, the poor man. Jess was instantly ashamed. How could she be angry with her husband when he might be seriously hurt, or even—?

No, she wouldn't allow herself to think the worst, but tears stung her eyes. Tears for Alan. Tears of self-pity.

Hoping Reece hadn't noticed them, she dashed at her face with the sleeve of the shirt he'd given her.

'Would you like your drink?'

She shook her head. She was past needing a drink. What she needed now was a miracle. She needed to be magically whisked away from this isolated, outback homestead. She knew Reece was doing his best and she was grateful. Truly. But how could a lonely bachelor cattleman deliver her baby? She wanted to be safely in Cairns with a midwife and a ward full of nurses...doctors on standby...

'Did you get through to the Flying Doctor?'

'Yes.'

'Is he on his way?'

Sympathy shone in Reece's dark eyes. 'With all this rain, they can't risk trying to land on our boggy airstrip.'

A surge of hot panic ripped through her now. 'What does that mean? I'll have to wait for an ambulance?'

He dropped his gaze and looked uncomfortable.

'Tell me there's an ambulance on its way,' Jess pleaded.

'Yes,' he said at last. 'A policeman is coming from Gidgee Springs and the ambulance from Dirranbilla.'

She sensed there was more bad news. 'But... what are you not telling me?'

Reece grimaced. 'The creeks are coming up fast.'

'So they might not make it?'

'It's…possible…'

This time, when Jess felt her face crumple, she didn't even try to be brave. What was the point? Everything was stacked against her. First a terrible accident, then her labour starting in the middle of nowhere. And now, no chance of help.

She and her baby were going to die.

All alone out here.

'Hey, Jess.'

She felt Reece's hand on her arm.

'It's OK,' he soothed. 'You're going to be OK.'

'I'm not,' she wailed. 'I don't know how to do this and neither do you.'

'I know how to deliver calves.' He gave a shrugging smile. 'And there's no need to panic. I've talked to a telehealth on-call doctor and he's told me what to do. He's on standby to talk me through step by step if I need help.'

'Oh, terrific. So I can have my baby by remote control and a tele—'

Her words were cut off as the urge to push crashed back with a vengeance. She screwed up her face and clenched her teeth to stop herself from screaming. She so-o-o wanted to push, but she couldn't forget the dire warnings from the antenatal teacher about not pushing too soon. Oh, God, how could she *not* push?

It was too hard to hold back.

'Can you see the baby's head?' she groaned.

'Would you like me to check?'

Exhausted already, Jess nodded, all pretence at modesty gone. If Reece could see the head she wouldn't keep fighting. She'd give in to the urge to push.

She watched his face as he cautiously lifted the shirt, saw his dark eyes widen and his Adam's apple ripple in his throat.

'What?' she demanded. 'What's happening down there?'

'Your baby has dark hair.'

Really?

In spite of everything, Jess felt her mouth tilt in a tremulous smile. The baby was a real little person. It had dark hair. She felt an unexpected spurt of excitement.

She looked at Reece, surprised by the emotion

shimmering behind his smile. The poor man hadn't asked to be thrown into this situation, and he was doing his best. She realised he'd spread a waterproof on the bed and he'd set up a tray with items from the medicine chest. He was a stranger, doing everything he could for her and for her baby.

She felt a rush of gratitude. 'Thanks for being here, Reece. If the baby's a boy I'll name him after you. And I'll—'

Once again, she was overtaken by an incredible force and every cell in her body urged her to give in to it. She was dimly aware that Reece was spreading more towels on the bed and taking something out of the medical chest. She heard the snap of sterile gloves.

There was nothing she could do but push.

And push.

And pu-u-u-sh.

'You're doing brilliantly,' Reece coaxed. 'The baby's shoulders are almost there now. Everything's happening just the way it's supposed to. Good girl. You're fabulous. That's it. Another push.'

'I can't.'

Exhausted, Jess sank back against the pillows. She couldn't push again. She didn't have the strength.

'Honestly, your baby's almost here,' Reece said again. 'Don't give up now, Jess. I can see its face. It's a real little cutie.'

'That's nice,' she said wearily.

But next moment, she was gripping her knees and pushing again, assisted, thank heavens, by another contraction.

'That's it, Jess. Here it comes. Good girl!'

Face screwed tight with the effort of another huge push, Jess felt the baby slip from her and she heard Reece's shout of triumph.

She fell back, panting, hardly daring to believe it was over so soon. Two breaths later, she asked, 'Boy or girl?'

'Well… I'm not sure about calling her Reece.'

'A girl?'

He was grinning from ear to ear. 'A perfectly beautiful baby girl.'

A girl. In the sudden lull, Jess felt exhausted

and strangely devoid of emotion. Secretly, she'd hoped for a girl, but she'd been so sure she was having a boy. It took a moment or two to adjust.

She closed her eyes, suddenly weary and drifting towards sleep.

'Waaaa!'

At that tiny, lusty yell, Jess's eyes whipped open and her heart gave a leap of joy, her exhaustion vanished in a blink. She struggled to sit. 'How is she? Is she all right?'

'She has all her fingers and toes. I'm no doctor, but she looks perfect to me.'

Jess wanted to see her, but before she could dig her elbows into the mattress and hoist herself upright Reece was at her side.

'Here,' he said gently.

She felt a warm weight on her chest and looked down. And discovered a miracle. Her baby daughter. Red and perfect, with a scrunched-up face. 'Hey, little girl.'

Her baby's skin was still shiny and wet, but she was so cute. She had tiny little fingers and toes with the sweetest little transparent nails. And she had the most exquisite, perfect, tiny ears. And her nose was tiny and perfect too, and so was her mouth. And her eyes. And her hair.

'Reece, she's utterly gorgeous.'

Looking up, she saw the silver sheen of tears in his eyes. He gave her an embarrassed, lopsided smile. 'Congratulations.'

'Congratulations to you too. You were brilliant.' Jess felt suddenly overwhelmed with gratitude. Everything had happened so quickly and, if it hadn't been for Reece, her baby might have been born on the edge of a dirt track out in the rain.

Now, this simple room, miles from anywhere, felt like the most wonderfully safe and comforting haven in the world.

'Thank you,' she said softly.

Somehow, just saying 'thank you' felt totally inadequate, but she was scared that she might start to cry if she tried to express how she really felt.

'Let's get this around her to keep her warm.' Businesslike again, Reece tucked a mauve crocheted blanket around the baby's tiny body. 'Do you want to see if she's hungry?'

'I'll try, I guess.'

'Do you know what to do?'

'I think so.'

With his work finally done, Reece stepped out onto the veranda, and realised he was shaking. He'd never held a baby before, not even when he was a godfather attending his nephew's fancy christening in a Sydney cathedral. Now, tonight, he'd assisted in a total stranger's birth. The little creature had slipped from her mother into the world.

Into his hands.

He'd looked down into her little face, all red and wrinkled. He'd watched her open her eyes for the very first time, and he'd seen the tiny quivering tremble of her lip, a heartbeat before she opened her mouth to give her first cry.

And he'd lost his heart.

Completely.

Now, as he stood at the veranda railing, trying to get a grip on his galloping emotions, he told himself to man up. He felt as if his life had changed in some significant way, but the reality was, it hadn't changed at all.

In an hour or two, the police or the ambulance would probably get through. If not tonight, tomorrow, or the next day… Then, this mother and baby would be gone. Out of his life. He'd be back to living alone with his ageing father as he had for almost thirty years. Back to carrying out his duty on this vast, back-breaking cattle property. Back to worrying about his father's health. Back to visiting lonely spinsters if he wanted female company.

'What's happening in there?'

Reece turned as his father appeared at his elbow and cocked his head to the French doors, now discreetly shut with the curtains drawn.

'Jess had a baby girl.' Reece's voice was choked as he said this.

'Crikey. She doesn't muck around, does she? Is she going to stay?'

'Of course not. She'll want to get back to the coast as fast as she can.'

'Yeah. They never want to stay.' His dad released an unexpectedly heavy sigh. After a bit, he brightened. 'Can I see her?'

'She needs a little time alone. She's feeding the baby. It's late, Dad. Why don't you go to bed?'

'What about the Flying Doc?'

'I'm going to ring them again now.' Reece had followed the doctor's instructions faithfully, using sterile gloves and scissors from the specially supplied medical chest, and the placenta had come away easily—*thank God*—but he wanted to double-check that he hadn't overlooked anything.

'You want to put lights out on the landing strip?' his father asked. 'I'll get the tins from the shed.'

Reece blinked. This was the first cooperative gesture his dad had made in ages. Unfortunately, he couldn't make use of it. He shook his head. 'It's too wet for the plane to land.' He smiled. 'But I'm sure we could all use a cup of tea.'

Jess was too stirred to sleep. Part of her mind was constantly worrying about Alan, while the rest of her thoughts were leaping with excitement. And she couldn't close her eyes because she didn't want to stop gazing in awe at the tiny sleeping beauty beside her. Reece had helped her to bath the baby. She'd been nervous of the tiny body, as slippery as a frog, but he'd been calm and gentle and sure.

Jess had dried her then, and wrapped her in strips of sheeting, because they had no nappies, while Reece fashioned a makeshift cot by padding a drawer with blankets and setting it on two chairs beside Jess's bed.

So now the baby was right there, at eye level and touching close, which was perfect. And Jess had chosen her name—Rosie Millicent Cassidy.

'Millicent after my grandmother. And Rosie because it's a bit like Reece,' she'd announced as she'd sat, propped by a bank of pillows and sipping hot, sweet tea.

A dark red stain crept up Reece's neck. 'You know, you don't have to name her after me.'

'I don't feel obliged, but you did save us from the worst possible nightmare. And anyway, Rosie is a pretty name.'

Reece looked down at the sleeping baby. 'Actually, she looks a bit like a half-opened rose.'

Jess grinned. 'That's a very poetic comment. Not quite what I expected from a cattleman. But it's true. She's pink and a little bit crumpled still, and sort of folded like rose petals.'

He smiled and shook his head at her and their gazes linked for a shade too long. He had the loveliest dark chocolate eyes, and Jess thought, momentarily, *If only...* And then she was ashamed of herself.

Perhaps Reece noticed. He moved to the door. 'I'll say goodnight.'

'Goodnight, and thanks again. For everything.'

'If you need me, call. I won't be far away and I'm a light sleeper.'

Jess felt strangely alone after he'd left. Outside the rain had slowed to a fine, dripping drizzle. She finished her tea, set the mug aside and settled down in the bed. Her body was exhausted. She really should try to get some sleep before Rosie woke again.

She closed her eyes. The house was very quiet

and outside there was just a background whisper of rain. She hoped Alan was safely in an ambulance, speeding to a hospital. She had no idea where the nearest hospital might be. She wondered if he would need to be airlifted to the coast…and she wondered when she would be able to tell him about Rosie…

Perhaps she drifted off to sleep, but she roused quickly when she heard the swish of tyres in puddles, and then a vehicle pulling up outside. Footsteps and voices. Men speaking quietly and at some length.

Jess wondered if it was the police, or an ambulance. Had they come for her? She sat up and switched on a bedside lamp and, of course, she checked on Rosie, pressing her hand gently to the baby's back to make sure she was still warm and breathing. Rosie wriggled and made a snuffling protest.

'Sorry,' Jess whispered. 'Didn't mean to disturb you.'

Footsteps approached from down the hallway. A soft tap sounded on her door.

'Come in,' she called.

Reece appeared, wearing an unbuttoned shirt that hung loose over his jeans, giving a hint of his broad chest with a smattering of dark hair, and a finely tapered waist. 'Sergeant Bryant is here, Jess. He apologises for the late hour, but he'd like to speak to you.'

She was suddenly scared and she felt a little sick as the policeman stepped into the room. He didn't look threatening, however. He was middle-aged, balding and thickset and his expression was one of almost fatherly concern.

'Good evening, Mrs Cassidy.'

'Hello, Sergeant.'

He nodded towards the cot and smiled. 'I believe congratulations are in order.'

'Thank you.'

He stepped closer. 'She's a little sweetie, isn't she? It's been a big night for you.'

'It has rather.' Jess swallowed a nervous lump in her throat. 'Have—have you seen my husband?'

Sergeant Bryant dropped his gaze and cleared

his throat and in that moment Jess knew, even before he spoke.

'I'm so sorry,' he said.

'He's d-dead?'

'I'm afraid he is.'

At some primitive level, she had probably known all along, but until now she'd never allowed herself to think it was actually possible. But faced with the horrible truth, Jess felt strangely numb. She'd run the full gamut of her emotions tonight and it was almost as if there was nothing left to feel right at this moment…

She couldn't even squeeze out a tear, but she knew the grief would come…later…

'At some stage I'll need to talk to you about the accident,' the sergeant said. 'But I won't bother you tonight.'

She nodded.

'The rain's almost stopped, so I'm hoping that the ambulance will be able to get through in another few hours,' he went on. 'It will bring you back to Dirranbilla. You'll be able to see a doctor. And then we can talk.'

He looked into the cot again and his face creased in a soft smile and then he left her.

Jess lay dazed, unable to focus on anything except the news that in another few hours…she would be leaving. She would be starting a new life.

How strange… For a short space of time this simply furnished room had been a little sanctuary for her and for Rosie…a safe haven from the wild night…and from the real world where all her savings were lost and accidents happened and husbands died…

Reece had been so kind. He'd delivered Rosie so beautifully. But in another few hours…

She would be gone…and the cruel irony was, she would be a single mum, after all.

CHAPTER THREE

2/56 Mary Street, Edmonton, Cairns
3rd March
Dear Reece,
Once again, thank you, although I know thanks aren't enough. Rosie and I owe you our lives. I will write again properly when I have more time, but I wanted you to know that Alan's funeral was yesterday and I'm managing OK.

I thought you might like this photo of Rosie. She's growing already, isn't she?
Warmest wishes and masses of gratitude,
Jess.

2/56 Mary Street, Edmonton, Cairns
25th April
Dear Reece,
Thank you so much for the pink teddy bear

and the little sleep suit dotted with roses. They are so cute—and such a kind thought. I cried when they arrived. I should be sending you gifts. I owe you so much. One day, I promise I'll repay you.

At least I can tell you that Rosie is thriving. She's filling out nicely and she doesn't wake too often, although she sometimes takes a bit of settling, especially in the evenings. Still, I can't complain.

She's started smiling. You've no idea how cute her smiles are. Once she starts, she just keeps on smiling as if she thinks the whole world is hilarious.

Thanks again and warmest wishes,
Jess

4a/89 Potts Street, Redlynch, Cairns
16th June
Dear Reece,
Another big thank you from Rosie and me. What a lovely surprise to open your parcel and to find your note and the gorgeous board

books. Rosie loves picture books and these are perfect.

I showed her the cows and the pigs and the turkeys and told her all about your farm—not that I saw much. She squealed and crowed and bashed at the pages with her fat little fingers, which is her way of showing how much she loves something.

You're probably sick of seeing photos of her, but here's one more. You can see she's quite roly-poly now. Please ignore how I look. I was a bit tired that day and I hadn't washed my hair, but then, you've seen me at my worst, haven't you?

Reece, I hope all is well with you. You didn't actually say much in your concise and slightly cryptic note. Mind you, that's not a criticism. For ever in your debt,
Jess

REECE opened the door to his father's room—just a crack—and made sure the old man was sleeping peacefully. Satisfied, he went back to the kitchen, grabbed a beer from the fridge and snapped its lid. Tipping his head, he took a draught, letting the icy lager slide down his throat.

He pushed the flyscreen door and went through to the veranda, propped his elbows on the railing and stared out at the paddocks that stretched long and flat to the distant line of trees. He thought again about Jess.

She made out that she was fine in her letters, but something wasn't right—he was sure of it. To begin with, she had no computer or phone for sending emails, and now she'd changed her street address. On the surface, that was probably no big deal—although a single mum moving house with a young baby couldn't be a picnic—but it was the photo that really bothered him.

He took it again from his shirt pocket and stepped into a circle of light to examine it carefully. The baby Rosie was as roly-poly and cute as Jess claimed. Reece found himself smiling as he recognised the same features he'd first witnessed on the night she was born, now filling out.

But he was shocked by the change in the young

mother. Jess was so thin, with dark shadows under her eyes, and no sparkle to her smile. She'd claimed she was just tired, but to him she looked ill, or worried. Or both.

You've seen me at my worst.

Not so, Reece thought, remembering her flushed cheeks and bright eyes as she greeted her baby for the first time.

Admittedly, becoming a widow and a mother on the very same night would be a terrible strain for any woman, but he couldn't shake off the feeling that Jess Cassidy was carrying an extra burden.

On top of his worries about his father, it was enough to keep him awake long into the night.

At the first lull in the café's morning chaos, Jess gave in to her fear. Ducking out of her boss's line of sight, behind the big commercial refrigerator in the back kitchen, she rang the day-care centre.

'Alana, it's Jess Cassidy. I'm just ringing to check if Rosie is still OK?'

'She seems fine,' the young attendant assured her.

'Are you sure there's no sign of a temperature?'

Rosie had been fretful all night and Jess was terrified she was getting sick.

'No, Jess. I knew you were worried so I've kept an especially close eye on her. She's had a nice nap and she woke up quite happy.'

'Well, that's good to hear. She was so upset last night. All night.'

'Perhaps she's teething. I noticed she's been chewing on her fists.'

'That's probably it. I guess it's about time.'

'Jess!' roared a male voice. 'What the hell are you up to?'

Jess spun around to find Joel Fink, her boss, glaring at her. Last time she'd looked, he'd been at the far end of the café busily chatting up his favourite female customer. 'I—I had to make a quick phone call.'

'Not on my time and not on my phone.'

'It wasn't a social call,' Jess told him coldly, refusing to be cowed. 'I needed to ring the day-care centre.'

'My customers' needs come first. And *they* need you to stop chatting and to feed them.' Snatching the phone from her, he slapped an order onto the bench. 'Two serves of strawberry pancakes. Cream, no ice cream. Get cracking.'

Lips tightly compressed, Jess got to work. Pancakes. Again. She was heartily sick of cooking breakfasts and lunches. As a fully qualified chef, she found it a breeze to produce light fluffy pancakes, or perfectly scrambled eggs and crisply fried bacon. But after almost six months of this she was bored. Just the same, this part-time job, working four days a week from six-thirty till two, was keeping a roof over her head and it was keeping Rosie fed. With Cairns's growing unemployment problems, she knew she'd been lucky to get the work and she should be grateful.

It would help if her boss wasn't such a cranky tight-fist. Privately, Jess called him The Cell Warder—even the menus he chose were as unimaginative as prison food. But at least this café was in walking distance of her flat, and working on Cairns's seafront gave her occasional glimpses of palm trees and sparkling water. More importantly, the daytime working hours left her with afternoons and evenings free.

She needed to be with Rosie in the evenings. It was horrendously expensive having to put her into day-care for four days a week, but she couldn't bear to hand her over to strangers at night.

Flipping pancakes, she promised herself she'd go to extra trouble with her own dinner tonight.

Reece was frowning as he knocked on the door of flat No 4a. The frown was partly because he was unexpectedly nervous about seeing Jess again, but also because he didn't like the idea of her living in this shabby, almost squalid building with peeling paint and rusted downpipes and rubbish bins littering the footpath.

His spirits sank lower when no one answered his knock.

A neighbour leaned out of a grimy window to stare at him. He walked over to her. 'I'm looking for Jess Cassidy.'

The young woman blew cigarette smoke. 'She's at work.'

'Where does she work?'

'No idea.' She narrowed her eyes at Reece, showing her distrust of him and making it patently clear that she wouldn't tell him even if she knew. 'She's gone most weekdays, though.'

'Thank you,' he said with excessive politeness, but as he walked away his worries about Jess multiplied.

Why was she working nearly every day? And where was Rosie? When Jess had written that she was 'managing OK', he'd wondered if perhaps she had to be frugal, but he'd still pictured her at home with her baby, living comfortably, if carefully, on her husband's insurance money.

Of course, Jess's living conditions were none of his business. Truth was, he hardly knew Jess Cassidy, and yet he'd been present at an intensely personal, pivotal moment in her life. They'd been through an emotionally charged ordeal together, and when Rosie was born they'd shared an exhilarating triumph. He'd *felt* connected.

Four months later, he still felt connected. It was a big deal for a man with precious few connections.

When he came back at six-thirty he saw, to his relief, that a light was on in Jess's flat. He could hear music playing a soothing, bluesy tune, and tempting cooking aromas wafted through an open window.

The tension inside him loosened a notch. Seemed Jess was all right, after all.

When he knocked, the door opened slowly and Jess stood before him with Rosie balanced on her hip. He was conscious of her slim, pale arms wrapped around the baby. She was wearing faded jeans and a soft pink T-shirt, and her dark hair was twisted into a loose knot. She was definitely thinner than before and she looked tired. On the other hand, her daughter looked plump and thriving.

At first, Jess's expression was guarded, almost defensive, but then she recognised him and her mouth formed an O of surprise.

'Hello, Jess.'

Rosie cooed at him and Jess smiled cautiously.

'I was in town,' Reece explained. 'I had to bring my father to the hospital for tests. He's being kept in overnight and I thought I'd drop by, to say hello.'

'It good to see you.' Jess hitched the baby a little higher. 'I hope your dad's going to be all right.'

'Thanks. It's hard to say at this stage.' Reece was holding a bunch of flowers wrapped in lavender tissue, but he felt suddenly uncertain about the appropriateness of bringing flowers. They had looked so bright and appealing, sitting in a bucket on the footpath, but now he wondered if Jess would think he was trying to be romantic.

'Rosie looks well,' he said, proffering, instead, the brightly wrapped gift he'd bought for the baby. 'I thought she might like this.'

'Reece, you've already been so kind.' With an embarrassed, almost wincing smile, Jess stepped back. 'You'd better come in.'

It wasn't the most welcoming invitation, but he went in, anyway. The flat was small and simply furnished with a tiny, rudimentary kitchen, a small table, two chairs and a single blue sofa. A door led to what he assumed was a bedroom. Everything was very clean.

'Take a seat.' Jess pointed to the sofa.

Uncertain what to do with the flowers, Reece set them on the table and sat at one end of the couch while Jess sat at the other end with Rosie, balancing the baby and the gift in her lap.

'Look what Reece has brought for you,' she said in a deliberately cheery voice, and the baby's hands swiped and patted at the wrapping paper as Jess peeled it away.

'Oh, wow!' she exclaimed as the brightly coloured toy was revealed.

'I'm told it's a chime garden,' Reece said and almost immediately Rosie banged a bright purple flower and was rewarded by a few tinkling bars of a nursery rhyme.

The baby grinned, and banged another flower, releasing more music, and Jess's face broke into a lovely smile. 'How clever. It's absolutely gorgeous, Reece. And the perfect toy for her age.'

Her green eyes sparkled—yes, her eyes were definitely green—and Reece realised that this was why he'd come: to reassure himself that she hadn't forgotten how to smile. She looked so heart-stoppingly pretty when her eyes lit up.

There was an awkward silence as they sat a metre apart and watched Rosie play with her new toy.

'How have you been, Jess?'

'Fine, thanks.' She tweaked a curl on her baby's head. 'Honestly. I hope you haven't been worrying about me.'

'No, not at all.'

Another awkward silence.

'Where are you staying?' Jess asked. 'Do you have friends in Cairns?'

'Not really. I'm booked into a pub down on the waterfront.'

'Nice.'

'Yes, it's fine. Close to the hospital.'

Rosie grabbed at her mother's nose and squealed with glee. Jess laughed, and then, suddenly, she asked, 'Would you like to stay for dinner?'

'No, no. I just dropped in for a quick hello. I don't want to impose on you.'

'I've made a chicken casserole.' Before he could answer, she hurried on. 'You must allow me to feed you, Reece, after everything you've done for me.'

He remembered her letters. *I owe you so much. One day, I promise I'll repay you.*

'Your cooking certainly smells very good,' he said.

'That's settled, then. It's all ready.' Jess smiled again and then she stood and set the baby down on a rug on the floor, putting the chime garden beside her, as well as the teddy bear he'd sent and a rattle. But as soon as she was down Rosie complained, waving her arms and throwing herself down and crying.

Jess sighed. 'I'm afraid she's always super grizzly and needy at this time of day.'

'Would she let me hold her?'

'I'm sure she'd love it. I'll check the dinner.' As Jess headed for the stove her pink mouth tilted into yet another smile.

Reece swallowed nervously as he looked down at the small, angry infant. His offer to pick her up had felt like the right thing to do, but now he was somewhat in awe of this writhing, small creature. He knew zilch about babies. He guessed they were probably like dogs, able to sense a person's fear. Sure enough, when he picked Rosie up, she stiffened as she stared at him.

At the same moment, a knock sounded on the door.

'Gosh,' Jess exclaimed as she set the hot casserole dish on a cane mat. 'I hardly ever have visitors, and now I have two in one night.'

What lousy timing, she thought as she slipped off the oven gloves. Now that she'd recovered from the shock of finding Reece on her doorstep, she'd even managed to shove aside the awkwardness she'd felt remembering her labour and everything poor Reece had been exposed to that night. With those thoughts carefully blocked, she was actually looking forward to sharing her dinner with him.

Apart from the fact that she owed him so much,

the past four months had been lonely, with hardly any time for catching up with her friends. Then again, her friends were mostly childless and always on the go at parties, or yachting weekends, or working overtime to 'get ahead'. But although Jess missed them, another visitor now would upset her dinner plans—there were only two chairs.

Someone would have to sit on the sofa.

She sent Reece an apologetic eye-roll as she went to answer the door, and her stomach tightened when she saw two strange, beefy and unsmiling men.

'He-hello,' she said uncertainly.

'Mrs Cassidy?'

'Yes.'

'Is your husband home?'

'No.' A cold shiver snaked over Jess's skin. 'My husband passed away several months ago.'

'I'm sorry to hear that.' The speaker was bald with bushy eyebrows and he looked momentarily wrong-footed. Recovering quickly, he shot a suspicious glance past Jess to Reece, who was standing a few feet behind her, holding Rosie.

Jess noticed, irrelevantly, that the baby looked amazingly tiny in Reece's strong, manly arms.

Facing her visitors again, she held her head higher. The fact that she was a widow alone with a handsome male guest was none of this stranger's business.

'I'm here to represent Tighe's Electrics,' he said.

Jess frowned. 'Electrics? My electricity's fine, thanks. Everything's fine.'

'I'm referring to your electrical white goods.' The man's tone held a hint of menace and he leaned forward to peer through the doorway into her tiny kitchen. 'You have a fridge and a washing machine and dryer and you've received communications from us regarding them.'

'No, I haven't.' Jess felt suddenly sick. 'I haven't heard anything about white goods. But I've moved quite a few times this year, and my mail has been messed around.'

'If you have a problem with the Post Office, that's nothing to do with me.' The man on her doorstep looked unsympathetic and waved an official-looking document under her nose. 'I've been authorised to repossess these items.'

Jess swayed against the door frame. 'You can't. I—I don't understand. My husband paid cash for them.'

He shook his head.

'Alan was absolutely definite. There must be a mistake.' Jess hoped she sounded convincing, but she sensed this was another battle she was almost certainly going to lose.

She'd had so much bad news in the past few months. So many things that Alan had kept hidden from her, including huge debts on two credit cards. She'd even discovered that he'd cashed in his life insurance, leaving her with nothing but a massive debt.

Until now, she'd been grateful that she'd at least found a job to pay for rent and food and the minimum repayments on all these other debts. Beyond that, her prize possessions were her transistor radio and her bed, plus the refrigerator and washing machine.

'Excuse me,' rumbled a deep voice behind her.

Jess jumped. She'd momentarily forgotten about Reece, and now she was flooded with wincing embarrassment. What must he think?

'There seems to be a problem,' he said. 'Perhaps I can help.'

Instinctively, Jess shook her head. Reece had already gone above and beyond the call of duty for her.

'Too late,' the man on the doorstep said, totally unconcerned. 'I have orders to repossess. Today. No more chances.'

'I can write a cheque,' Reece replied firmly.

A bushy eyebrow lifted. 'Sorry, mate. As I said, time's run out.' Switching his attention to Jess, he said, 'We can do this the easy way or the hard way. You let me take these items now, or I can come back with the police.'

'I have no intention of fighting you.'

Chin high, with as much dignity as she could muster, Jess stepped back as the fellow barged through the doorway.

'Come on, Fred,' he said over his shoulder. 'Let's get this lot into the truck.'

'Hang on,' Jess protested. 'There's food in the fridge.'

'I'll empty it out.'

'No, you won't.' With sudden, fierce determination, she pushed past him. She was humiliated and devastated, but she sure as hell wasn't going to let this bullying oaf walk all over her. 'I'll take my food out, thank you very much.'

Lips compressed, she wrenched the fridge door open and began to remove its contents, setting the items neatly and efficiently on the draining board. Eggs, butter, milk, cheese…a plastic container of home-made stewed apple, another of chicken stock…

Watching her, Reece wanted to roar with rage. He'd never felt so furious and so helpless. It was probably just as well he was holding the baby, or he might have shoved an angry fist in these guys' smug faces. He was so maddened to see Jess treated like this. He couldn't imagine the circumstances the poor girl had been left in.

When the refrigerator was emptied, Jess came

over to him, her face tight and pink, but composed. 'Thanks for looking after Rosie.'

'No problem.'

She took her baby from him and hugged her close. 'At least no one can take you,' she murmured, dropping a kiss on the little girl's downy head.

Out in the street her refrigerator was being loaded into a truck and for the first time her eyes brimmed with tears.

Reece's throat tightened on a painful rock. 'Will you be able to manage?'

'Oh, sure. I'll have this sorted tomorrow.'

He knew she was covering a host of worries, and she didn't want to admit she was in trouble, which made it hard for him to help.

'I'll duck out and get some ice,' he suggested. 'Then you can keep things cold in the sink overnight.'

She nodded without quite meeting his gaze. 'That's a good idea. Thanks.' Then she looked up at him, her green eyes shimmering, and she gave him a brave but tremulous smile.

Reece felt as if he'd swallowed razor blades.

* * *

The truck was gone by the time he arrived back with a bag of ice. He couldn't see Jess, but there was a soft light coming from behind the bedroom curtains and she'd left the front door open. He guessed she was settling the baby to sleep, so he entered the flat quietly and glared at the dusty gap in the corner where the fridge had been. Then he placed the ice in the sink and packed the fridge items in with it.

He noticed that the casserole dish was back in the oven and the radio had been turned down low.

Jess came tiptoeing into the room, a finger to her lips. 'I think she's down for the count,' she whispered, and then she picked up the flowers he'd brought. 'I haven't even thanked you for these gerberas. They're lovely, Reece. So bright and cheerful.'

Once again, he felt sure the flowers were totally wrong.

'I don't think I have a vase,' Jess said. 'I might have to put them in a jug.'

He held up a bottle of wine. 'While I was out,

I decided we could use a drop of vino to go with the chicken.'

Jess brightened. 'So you still want to stay?'

'You invited me, didn't you?'

'Of course.' Her smile lingered as she quickly found tumblers for the wine, put the flowers in a green glass jug and set the table with cheery red mats. The bright colours made the fridge-less kitchen seem less depressing.

Jess served up the fragrant meal and they sat, just a little self-consciously.

'This is sensational,' Reece said as he tasted the chicken.

'Yes, it's one of my favourites.'

'So you like cooking?'

'Sure. It's my job.'

'Really?'

'I'm a chef.'

He knew so little about her. She was the girl he'd found on the side of the road. A girl in trouble, a girl still in trouble. He ate in silence, caught up in his thoughts.

'You're not huge on conversation, are you?'

He looked up to find Jess watching him, her eyes dancing with private amusement.

'Sorry. I was thinking.'

'About your father?'

'Partly.' He couldn't deny that he was haunted by the image of his dad looking lost and intimidated in the big city hospital. He would duck back there soon to make sure the old man was settled for the night. 'I was also thinking about you.'

'Don't worry about me.' She picked up her glass. 'This is a very fine wine.'

Reece couldn't let her change the subject so easily. 'Sorry, Jess, but I can't help being concerned. You're not in trouble, are you?'

'No, I'm absolutely fine. I have a job, and I'm managing. Honestly.'

'Are you in a position to buy a new fridge and washing machine?'

'Of course.'

He was sure she was lying.

'Look,' Jess said tightly. 'I don't want to talk about money tonight. I'm sick of thinking about money and bills. I'll deal with that tomorrow. I want to channel Scarlett O'Hara. Another day and all that, and I'll work something out. But tonight, my baby's asleep, I have adult company, and we're drinking a very good wine. I'd very much like to enjoy it.'

With a wave of her glass, she gestured to the table and then to him and her mouth quirked into a shy smile. 'Believe me, this is an unexpected but gratefully appreciated luxury.'

Reece found himself returning her smile. Truth was, this was a luxury for him too. Dining with a pretty girl who happened to also be a fabulous cook made a brilliant change from his own bland cooking and his father's increasingly dour company.

Just the same... Jess hadn't just lost a husband—she'd lost a life partner, a support base. 'I know you don't want to talk about it, but this must have been hard for you, managing on your own. Do you have support? Friends? Family?'

'Yes, Reece.'

Her reply was too quick, but he knew she'd hate it if he pushed her any further.

She smiled again as she sipped her wine. 'So tell me… If you could be absolutely anywhere in the world right now, where would you like to be?'

Here, he almost said, and then checked himself just in time. She would be shocked if she knew how much he was enjoying this meal and her company.

'Come on,' Jess prompted. 'Where would you choose? City or country?'

Reece shrugged. 'City, I guess. I wouldn't mind a city break.'

'In summer or winter?'

'Maybe winter. A total change from the tropics. Possibly with snow.'

'Manhattan in January,' she suggested, her green eyes alight.

'Sounds about perfect.' He pictured her on a crowded Manhattan street. Saw her against a background of yellow taxis and skyscrapers. She would be wearing a long coat with a bright scarf at her throat and there'd be snowflakes in her dark hair. The image was entrancing.

'What about you?' he remembered to ask. 'Where would you like to be?'

Jess's eyes were lit by a gratifying sparkle. 'I wouldn't say no to Manhattan. As long as I could afford to buy really trendy clothes. But...' she cocked her head to one side '...I guess it depends... If I had Rosie with me, I might choose the beach. Not a North Queensland beach. I wouldn't want stingers or crocodiles. Somewhere with surf and sandcastles and wading pools.'

Now, he was picturing Jess in a bikini.

Damn, he was a fool.

Later...Jess washed the dinner dishes in the laundry tub, because the kitchen sink was now packed with ice and the contents of her fridge. Of course, she wouldn't let Reece help her with the dishes, but after she'd sent him away, she felt depressed.

She missed him already, which was crazy. He wasn't hers to miss. He was an out-of-town cattleman passing through, but now that he was gone she couldn't hold off facing her problems. She had absolutely no money to spare. As it was, sharing her dinner with Reece meant that she'd be eating baked beans on toast by the end of the week. But how on earth could she manage without a fridge and a washing machine?

She'd been trying so hard to keep her head above water, but now she felt overwhelmed by debt and black despair. She was drowning.

It had been so hard to hide her desolation from Reece, but she'd been determined. She couldn't fall apart in front of him. Not again.

On the upside, they'd shared a very pleasant evening. Sitting across the dinner table from him, she'd found herself mesmerised by his dark brown eyes and the clean lines of his cheekbones. But, of course, she had to stop any hint of dreamy thoughts.

To begin with, Reece hadn't shown the slightest hint that he was in any way romantically interested in her, and even if he had she couldn't allow herself to become involved with another man. Not for ages, quite possibly not ever.

Not with these debts hanging over her head. She could never go into another relationship so encumbered. Her goal now was a stable, happy life for Rosie, and it was up to her to provide it. It was going to take years to get her finances back on track, and till then she couldn't allow herself to be distracted by another guy, no matter how kind, or heroic, or attractive.

Anyway, besides her debt worries, falling for Alan had taught her many lessons—enough to make her doubt men and to doubt her own judgement when it came to making romantic choices.

She'd been totally taken in by Alan's good looks and charming manner, and, after they'd married, he'd talked her into setting up her dream restaurant. He'd had it all planned. He would help to finance the venture. Jess would be head chef and he would be manager and together they'd attract fame and fortune.

In reality, Jess had worked her butt off in the kitchen, while Alan swanned about in the dining room, greeting their customers like bosom buddies, regaling them with stories they didn't want to hear and drinking their wine. As a business manager, he'd been utterly hopeless. After six months, Jess had been so worried, she'd sat up one night until dawn trying to make sense of their finances.

What she'd found had appalled her. Alan had never invested his own money, and now they weren't keeping up with repayments on the loan, and other bills had also gone unpaid. Their business had gone under three months later.

It was the beginning of a disastrous pattern. Looking back, it was hard to believe that Alan had twice managed to convince her that they'd get it right the next time.

Remembering it all now, Jess felt such a mix of sorrow and regret, *and* anger, but a good swag of the anger was directed at herself. She'd been too easily sucked in by Alan's charm and his hollow promises.

She'd spent three years trying to believe in him.

In the future, she *had* to be wiser, and her safest bet was to rely on no one. Go it alone. She'd watched her mother limp from one disastrous relationship to another, and she'd vowed she'd never follow her example.

Now, she tiptoed into the bedroom she shared with Rosie. The old second-hand cot didn't look as scratched and ugly in the soft pink glow of the rabbit-shaped night lamp. She could see Rosie lying on her side, her hair, lighter now, and soft as a cloud, her little hands loose and relaxed, a bubble of milk on her lower lip. As always, Jess felt her heart swell with love. Love sweet and painful and more powerful than anything she'd imagined.

We'll be OK, she silently promised her daughter. *I can do this. I'm a hard worker and in time, I'll clear these debts and I'll make a wonderful life for us.*

Without a man.

CHAPTER FOUR

AFTER the doctor left, Michael and Reece Weston eyed each other uncertainly.

There'd been good news and not so good. At least, the results of the tests were better than Reece had feared. His father didn't need invasive procedures and he didn't have to stay in hospital. But there were signs of congestive heart failure and, chances were, problems like fatigue, shortness of breath and swelling of his legs would get worse in the not too distant future.

The doctor had increased the blood-pressure medication, and he'd suggested lifestyle modifications. He'd also strongly advised that Michael should consider moving from Warringa to a retirement village in Cairns.

'There's a very good place with a nursing home

attached,' the doctor had said, and he'd asked a social worker to provide them with pamphlets.

Now, with a disgusted grunt, Reece's father flicked the pamphlet off his bedspread, letting it flutter to the floor. 'If they think I'm going into one of those damn places, they've another think coming.'

'You'd be able to see a doctor regularly,' Reece suggested carefully.

His father simply scowled. 'I couldn't stand being holed up with a lot of dreary old folk, all of them losing their marbles together.'

Bending down, Reece picked up the pamphlet. It showed pictures of healthy, happy seniors all neatly dressed and smiling, and enjoying a range of activities—art classes, walking groups, golf, gardening...

'If anything happens...' Reece frowned as he chose his words carefully. 'If there's a medical emergency, you'd be looked after straight away. Think how long it would take a doctor to get out to Warringa.'

'I don't care. I'm happy to die there,' his father

announced emphatically. 'I've lived there all my flaming life and I don't plan to leave my home now.'

It was hard for Reece to hear his father speak so casually about death. But they'd lived together, just the two of them, for so long that, of course, he wasn't surprised. His dad had only ever known the red dust and wide open skies and the isolation that came with outback life. He couldn't honestly imagine Michael Weston settling into an art class or going for a walk in the Cairns Botanical Gardens with a bunch of chattering old folk.

His dad's life had been tough and lonely—driving mobs of cattle across vast tracks of wild country, coping with droughts and floods and fires. His father's one attempt at marriage had been an abject failure, and after the divorce Michael Weston had stubbornly turned his back on society.

Reflecting on this now, Reece found himself remembering another time, when he was five years old, when his dad had brought him here to this same hospital in Cairns to visit his mother and to meet his new baby brother. His heart still ached when he remembered his mother in bed, looking pale and lovely in a frilly pink bed jacket.

'Your little brother's called Anthony,' she'd told Reece as he'd peeped shyly into the cot.

'But we'll call him Tony,' his dad had added.

His mother had snapped. 'No, we won't.'

Reece could still remember the fear that had gripped him as he'd become aware, yet again, of his parents' tight-lipped animosity. Tension had bristled in the air around him as he'd stared into the cot at his brother. He'd been hoping for a playmate—he'd seen baby calves that could stagger onto four legs within minutes of birth—and he was disappointed that his brother was so tiny and helpless. Anthony—or Tony—did nothing but sleep.

'Will Anthony be able to play with me when he wakes up?'

His mother had laughed at this, and then she'd cried. She'd cried hard and long.

In the end, Reece had never played with his little brother, not unless he counted their awkward attempts to kick a football around a backyard, during his infrequent visits south. His mother had never brought the new baby home to Warringa. She'd stayed in Cairns.

In later years, Reece learned that she'd had post-natal depression, but even when the depression lifted she hadn't come home. She'd moved back to Sydney, keeping Tony with her, and leaving Reece with his father.

So…apart from his years away at boarding school, Reece had shared his father's solitary life, and he understood how a man could reach a point where he accepted isolation and loneliness as his destiny.

He was pretty damn near that point himself. It was certainly too late to expect his old man to change.

But accepting this didn't ease Reece's current dilemma. If he was to manage Warringa, including this year's cattle muster, he couldn't also look after his father. He was going to need help, and he was going to have to find that help fast.

To Jess's surprise, Reece was waiting outside the café when she finished work. He was on the footpath, standing with his hands sunk in his jeans pockets and a bulky shoulder propped against the trunk of a coconut palm. Filtered sunlight lent his black hair the sheen of crow's feathers. With the additional bonus of his coal-dark eyes, his craggy cheekbones and a faint shadow of beard, he looked frighteningly attractive.

She didn't want an attractive man in her life, so it was perverse of her to care that this hunky guy always seemed to catch her looking her worst. This time, she was in her chef's gear with her hair yanked back off her face, unattractive trousers, a smeared white jacket and sensible lace-up shoes.

'G'day,' Reece said with a slow smile.

'Hello, Reece.'

His smile lingered. 'Has anyone told you, you make a mean steak sandwich?'

Jess's jaw dropped. 'When did you eat at this café?'

'My father and I had lunch here.'

She remembered now—in the middle of the lunch-time rush, her boss had grudgingly passed on a customer's compliments.

'Best steak sandwich he's ever had,' Joel had grunted, but Jess had been mega busy at the time and hadn't given it another thought.

Now, she couldn't help wondering why Reece was still hanging around. He wasn't stalking her, surely?

'So I guess that means your dad's out of hospital,' she said quickly. 'How is he?'

'Not too bad, thanks. Right now, he's relaxing at the motel, enjoying the air-conditioning and the pay TV.'

'I can imagine. I'm glad he's OK.'

'Well, he's not totally OK.' Reece switched his gaze to the distant horizon where the calm waters of the Coral Sea met the sky. Blue on blue. He turned back to her. 'Were you heading somewhere now?'

'I'm off to the day-care centre to collect Rosie.'

'Walking?'

Jess hesitated. She liked Reece—probably liked him too much—and she certainly appreciated everything he'd done for her and for Rosie, but she had to be careful. She wasn't sure if he was trying to chat her up, and she couldn't afford to give him the wrong idea.

To her surprise, his dark eyes took on a nervous flicker. His throat worked and he shrugged awkwardly. 'If that sounded like a pick-up line, it wasn't what I meant.'

Gosh, had he read her mind? Feeling just a little confused, she smiled. 'The day-care's this way. Let's go.'

Reece fell in beside her and, after a short stretch of silence, he said, 'I was wondering if you planned to shop for the white goods today.'

Ah...so his interest was purely practical. Jess squashed a ridiculous ripple of disappointment. 'No, I won't be shopping for those things today.' The sad truth was that, for the time being, she would have to make do with a picnic ice chest and hand washing or the Laundromat, but she was too proud to admit this to Reece.

Now, however, he stopped abruptly, and once again he shoved his hands deep into his pockets.

They were standing near the fence of a vividly tropical garden, and afterwards, whenever Jess remembered this occasion, she could recall every detail as if the moment had been imprinted on her.

The hum of traffic half a block away…

The heady scent of jasmine…

The industrious buzzing of bees…

Reece's nervousness and the way his face pulled into an awkward grimace…

'Is something the matter, Reece?'

His funny-sad smile should not have sent her insides tumbling.

'I've a suggestion I'd like to put to you,' he said. 'I think it could help you, but I don't know if you'll like it.'

Immediately, Jess was shaking her head. 'If you're thinking about lending me money, forget it. I couldn't possibly accept.'

'It's not a loan.'

She frowned. 'What's your suggestion, then?'

'A job.'

'But…I've got a job.'

'I know, so this may not suit, but maybe if I explain…'

Jess nodded, as curious as a fish rising to the bait. 'OK.'

Reece swallowed. 'The thing is, I need someone to keep an eye on my father, so I'm going to have to hire some help.'

'A nurse?'

'No, not really a nurse. More like a housekeeper. Someone to cook and look after the house and just be there at the homestead. If I can't find anyone suitable, my only alternative is to hire a contract mustering team and let them take care of the cattle business while I look after Dad. I can't possibly manage both jobs.'

'I—I see.' Jess certainly sympathised with his dilemma.

Reece cleared his throat. 'I'd pay you well.'

Her insides were fluttering like leaves in a high wind. 'And this—this housekeeper—would she live at the homestead?'

'Yes, but it's a big house. If you came, you'd have your own room and bathroom and a sleepout right beside you that could be Rosie's nursery.'

Obviously, he'd thought it all out.

And Jess couldn't deny she was sorely tempted. Wow…if she took this job, she wouldn't have to pay for her food and rent, *and* she'd still be earning money. She could make inroads on those awful debts…

It was incredibly tempting.

Too tempting.

Surely, it had to be a tempting trap.

Her mind raced, weighing up pros and cons. The financial benefits were very clear, and she would quite enjoy the housekeeping and cooking, and she wouldn't mind keeping an eye on Reece's dad.

On the downside, she would be living with Reece—and while she felt an unwise thrum of excitement at that thought, she knew she had to be sensible. Reece was so muscly and tantalisingly good-looking, *and* he was thoroughly nice, but his combined attributes presented a dangerous package.

Only last night, she'd reminded herself that she had to avoid this kind of man-trap. Going out there with Reece, living miles from anywhere, more or less alone with him, could be great fun, but it would also create all kinds of relationship dangers. She had to be sensible. Had to remember her plan to get on top of her problems before she risked another romance.

Reluctantly, Jess shook her head. 'I'm sorry, Reece. I think I'd rather stick to working in Cairns.'

'Of course.' Apart from the tightening of his jaw, she saw no hint of a negative reaction. So that was a good thing.

'It was a long shot.' His quick smile didn't quite reach his eyes. 'Worth a try.'

'Thanks for thinking of me.'

He shrugged. 'No problem.'

Jess glanced down the street. The day-care centre was only three doors away and she nodded towards its sign, complete with pictures of teddy bears and wide-eyed dolls. 'I'd better collect Rosie.'

'Sure.'

'Reece, I hope everything works out for you. With your father and everything.'

'Oh, it'll be fine. Don't worry.'

'Please give him my regards.' Feeling inexplicably depressed, Jess stepped closer, lifted her face and pressed a hasty kiss to his jaw. Her lips met his masculine stubble and she had to fight a longing to linger. 'I'd better go, but I'll keep in touch.'

'Yes, do that. Give Rosie a cuddle from me.'

'I will.'

As she turned and hurried away her eyes filled with tears. How crazy was that? She knew she'd made a wise decision.

And yet…

If I was working in a homestead, Rosie wouldn't have to be in day-care. I could have her with me every day, all the time.

But no…she couldn't give in to immediate regrets. She had to be strong, had to stick to her goals of independence and eventual security.

Then again…taking that job would be a way of repaying Reece.

This thought brought Jess up with an appalled jolt.

Was she being horribly selfish? Reece was facing a dilemma. He needed help with caring for his father, in the same way that she'd needed his help on the night Rosie was born.

He hadn't hesitated to help them, and yet she'd dismissed him so coolly...

Poised in the doorway of the day-care centre, Jess turned and looked back down the street. Reece was striding away on long legs and he'd almost reached the corner.

She started to run.

It was for the best, Reece told himself as he walked away and valiantly ignored the gutted hollowness inside him.

Hiring Jess to work at Warringa was a crazy thought anyway. Sure, she was a great cook, and she almost certainly needed a chance to save money, but taking her to Warringa was a risk. Already, after she'd spent one night in his home, he'd found himself caring about her and her little daughter. He could become too attached if they stayed for six months or a year or more before they left.

And Jess and Rosie *would* leave.

Reece had absolutely no doubts about that. He'd learned lessons from his mother's desertion as well as a few failed attempts when girlfriends had found his home too isolated. He knew Jess had been sensible when she knocked back the offer, and, despite the lingering imprint of her soft lips on his skin, he was grateful.

He'd go straight to an employment agency and find a sensible woman with good credentials. Failing that, he'd hire a contract mustering team and he'd take care of his dad himself. One way or another he'd get around this problem and—

'Reece!'

Jess's call zapped through him like an electric charge. He turned to find her running down the footpath and, to his dismay, his heart began to pound.

He began to run too. 'Is something wrong?' he called as he neared her. 'Is Rosie OK?'

Jess shook her head and stood panting and

breathless. 'This isn't about Rosie,' she said, even-tually. 'I—I've had second thoughts. About the job. I'd like to help you out.'

Reece willed himself to remain outwardly calm while his heart thrashed.

'I'm sorry I turned you down,' she said. 'I don't know why I hesitated.'

'Warringa is very isolated.'

'I know that, but I wouldn't mind. Alan and I were planning to live in Gidgee Springs, so Rosie and I would have been in the outback anyhow. And—' She flashed a shy smile. 'And I owe you.'

'No, you don't.'

'I do, Reece. You've done so much for me.'

'This isn't about gratitude. It's a practical job offer.'

'Yes…' Jess nodded. 'And I'd be very pleased to accept the offer.'

Was she sure about this? Reece didn't dare to ask. She might change her mind.

Ignoring the loud pealing of warning bells, he said, 'That's wonderful.'

* * *

'Jess Cassidy?' scowled Reece's father. 'Isn't that the girl who had the baby?'

'Yes. She's also an excellent cook and house-keeper.'

His father's eyes narrowed shrewdly. 'So you're keen on her, after all. I thought you were.'

'Course I'm not. I'm hiring her to take care of you.'

'I don't need taking care of.'

Reece sighed. 'OK. I'm not going to argue about this. You know I'll have to start mustering soon and I'll be a darned sight more relaxed if there's someone at the homestead with you.'

'A prison warder.'

'Hardly.'

'What about her baby?'

'Her name's Rosie and she'll be coming too, of course.'

'She'll be crying all night.'

'I don't think she cries much, but, anyway, I'll put her and Jess at the far end of the house, away from you. And I'll buy you ear plugs, or you can turn the television up. I'm sure Jess and Rosie won't bother you. You might even enjoy having a baby about the place.'

'I doubt it.' His father pulled a face. 'You were a terrible baby. Cried all the time.'

Reece sighed again. 'I'm sure Rosie's much better behaved than I was.'

'Gran, it's Jess. How are you?'

'I'm very well, dear. How are you? How's Rosie?'

'We're fine, thanks. Rosie's growing so fast. I wish you could see her.'

'I have the lovely photo you sent on my dressing table.'

Yes, it would be there along with the rest of her seven grandchildren. Sometimes it was hard for Jess to remember that she had to share her grandmother. Since her mum died, Gran was the only member of her close family still alive. But Gran had three sons Jess had only met once or twice and six grandchildren besides Jess. Gran and her sons' families all lived at the Gold Coast at the opposite end of Queensland from Cairns.

After Alan died, Jess had considered moving there, but she couldn't afford the travel and removal costs.

'I'm ringing to tell you that I have a new job,' Jess said.

'Oh. Is it a good one? Are you happy?'

'I think it's perfect, actually. I'm going to be working on a cattle property, as a housekeeper and cook.'

'A cattle property? In the outback?'

'Yes, it's the property where Rosie was born, actually.'

'I see. So you'll be working for that wonderful young man who helped you?'

'Yes. But I'm sure I didn't tell you he was wonderful.'

'But you really liked him.'

'Not in the way you're thinking.' She'd never been a very good liar. 'This new job is just that, Gran—a job.'

She wasn't like her mother, starting a new relationship with each new man she met, but she couldn't explain that to her grandmother without implying criticism of her mum, Gran's daughter.

At least her terms of employment were crystal clear in her own mind.

Jess was pleased about that.

Travelling down the track to Reece's homestead in broad daylight was very different from the other panicky trip through a rainy night. Today Jess had clear views of rolling grassy paddocks dotted with Brahman cattle, as well as the white egrets that so often accompanied them. She could see the dark lines of trees that marked the creek's winding progress, and there were red rocky ridges, long sloping plains and the smudge of blue hills in the distance.

It all felt like an adventure and she took in the views with fresh interest. Reece's ute had a dual cabin, so she was sitting in the back seat beside her dozing daughter, while Reece's father, Michael, was in the front, also napping, with his head lolling sideways.

In the very rear of the truck, along with Jess's gear, they carried a brand-new white cot and a matching white chest of drawers, as well as a high chair, a mosquito net and several packages of baby clothes.

'It gets cold out at Warringa in the winter,' Reece had warned as he piled extra sleep suits and several pairs of fluffy socks into the trolley.

Jess had protested, but he'd insisted on buying these things. 'Rosie has to be warm enough.' He'd also insisted on buying a lovely mobile to hang above the cot—animals made of brightly coloured felt: a purple and pink owl, a black and white zebra with a fiery red mane, a golden and brown lion and a bright pink pig. Jess was grateful for these lovely things, but she hoped she could eventually pay Reece for them. She was determined to hang on to her independence and she didn't want to be beholden.

As they approached the homestead, however, her excitement mounted. Outbuildings appeared—tractor sheds, stables, a windmill. Jess found herself sitting straighter, peering ahead, keen for another glimpse of the homestead.

They rounded a final bend and there was the house, a sprawling, low-set, timber Queenslander, painted white, with a faded red iron roof that was almost completely shaded by two massive old Moreton Bay fig trees.

Jess remembered the other time she'd arrived here—peering at the house through the rain, and seeing the lights shining on the veranda, then the semi-dark sanctuary of Reece's bedroom. Today, sheltered from the blazing sun, this house looked a little shabbier perhaps—certainly in need of new coats of paint—but unexpectedly welcoming just the same. In fact, to Jess, who'd spent her entire life living in cramped rented flats, arriving at Warringa felt like a dream come true. Dangerously so.

But she'd been planning to make a new start with Alan in the outback, and now she was doing it alone. This was her chance to get ahead and she had to get it right.

CHAPTER FIVE

'YOU'LL sleep in my room again tonight.'

Jess stared at Reece in puzzlement and prayed that she wasn't blushing.

'Just for one night,' he elaborated. 'The other rooms aren't quite ready for you and Rosie.'

'But—but—' *Far out.* She should be able to handle this simple situation without stammering, but the day's close proximity to Reece had apparently downsized her brain.

'But?' A dark eyebrow lifted as his mildly amused gaze seared her. 'Are you worried about where I plan to sleep?'

'Not really.' It was a lie. Where he planned to sleep was exactly what she needed to know.

'I'll swag down on the veranda. Same as last time.'

Of course. She should have known that. *Cringe.*

She hadn't really thought that Reece was angling for them to sleep together. He showed no sign that he found her attractive, and that was totally understandable after the way they met when she was as wet as a drowned rat and groaning in labour.

But should her employer be sleeping on the floor? It seemed wrong.

'Don't look so shocked, Jess.' His eyes flashed again. 'I've spent a good part of my life sleeping in swags out in the bush.'

'Yes, yes, of course you have.'

'Anyway,' he went on smoothly. 'Before we sort the bedrooms, let me show you the kitchen. We can put the kettle on.'

With Rosie chirping happily in her arms, she followed Reece's easy stride across a covered walkway lined with hanging baskets of rather bedraggled ferns to a smaller wooden building, which proved to be the kitchen.

'The separate kitchen is a hangover from the old days,' Reece explained as he filled a kettle and lit the gas. 'Everyone had wood stoves back then, and the theory was that if the kitchen caught fire, the rest of the house could still be saved.'

'It makes very good sense.' Jess looked about her. She wouldn't mind working in a separate domain. The room was rather plain, with no feminine decorative touches, but it was light and airy, with a bank of deep casement windows to catch the breezes. There was also a huge stove with two ovens, and masses of bench space, as well as a scrubbed pine table and chairs for everyday dining.

Once Rosie's high chair was in place with a few toys scattered about and various ingredients dotted about the work surfaces, it would look very homely. Jess could hardly wait to start work.

'And the pantry's through here,' Reece said.

Wide-eyed, she followed him into another room lined with shelves stacked with enough provisions to stock a small grocery store.

'Oh, wow!' she exclaimed with a huge grin. 'I. Am. In. Heaven.'

Reece gave a shocked laugh. 'You're easy to please.'

'Every cook dreams of having storage space like this.'

'You haven't seen the cold room yet.'

She gaped at him. 'There's a cold room too?'

'Right here.' He pushed open a heavy door.

'Oh, my God.'

'I know it's a bit confronting to meet half a beast hanging from a hook.'

But Jess had no qualms at all about the butcher-shop scenario. 'It's amazing. It's fabulous, Reece.' She was grinning. 'I think I'm in love.'

He switched his gaze to a far corner and scowled.

'With your kitchen setup,' she added hastily, cheeks burning.

'The baby will get cold if we stay in here too long,' he said, but he didn't meet her gaze as he opened the door for her.

Reece's father sat at the dining table, waiting for his dinner, a napkin already tucked into his shirt as he watched Jess mix Rosie's formula.

'What's wrong with mother's milk?' he asked, his jaw at a belligerent angle.

Jess winced, instantly defensive. The old man might have had a hard life, but he had no idea how hard it had been for her in those early weeks. She'd been so scared trying to care for her tiny newborn daughter on her own, and at the same time grappling with the shock of losing Alan while acquiring his mountainous debts.

She took a deep breath before she answered. 'I'm afraid I was too stressed after my husband died, and I just wasn't able to breastfeed.'

As Michael shook his head, unimpressed, Reece turned from the stove—he'd insisted on fixing dinner on this first night. 'Give the girl a break, Dad. What would you know about babies?'

Jess could have hugged him. Michael glared at them both, but after a while his face lost its sneer and he gave a sheepish shrug. 'Well…maybe you'll have better luck next time.'

'Oh, I very much doubt there'll be a next time.'

'Rubbish. You're bound to have a tribe of ankle biters, isn't she, Reece?'

Reece didn't grace this question with an answer, but continued stirring savoury mince at the stove, adding extra Worcestershire sauce. Jess was used to working with men in the kitchen, but she found it incredible that Reece managed to look even more intensely masculine and outdoorsy while he was working at the stove. She was beginning to suspect that his muscles and low-riding jeans were an indoor health hazard.

Her breathing would certainly be a whole lot steadier when this kitchen was her sole territory.

It was shortly after midnight when Rosie started crying.

Reece heard her wailing as he lay in his swag on the veranda, and then he heard the creak of a floorboard as Jess stepped out of bed. He heard Jess's soft whispers as she tried to hush the baby, and he pictured her lifting Rosie onto her shoulder, kissing the baby's soft pink cheek and jogging her lightly up and down, trying to rock her back to sleep.

Problem was, he'd spent far too much time today watching Jess with Rosie. He'd been entranced by the way her face softened whenever she looked at her baby, by the way her voice grew gentle and loving. He could have spent ages watching the way she cuddled Rosie close, showering her with soft, sweet kisses. It touched him deeply to witness such tender intimacy and selfless love…

No doubt a shrink would connect his newfound fixation with buried feelings of abandonment by his own mother.

Yeah…

Whatever…

When Rosie's crying continued, he left the swag and tiptoed through the house to make sure his father's bedroom door was closed, and for good measure, he closed the doors at the ends of the hallway as well.

He thought about knocking on Jess's door and offering to heat up a bottle. Imagined encountering Jess in her nightgown and thought better of it.

By the time he was back in his swag, lying with his hands stacked under his head and staring out at the starry sky, the house was silent again.

He heard the board creak as Jess climbed back into bed.

So that was that…time for sleep. Only one problem. When he closed his eyes, he was plagued by images of Jess in her nightgown, of the soft see-through fabric and moonlight outlining her slim, pale curves…fantasies of her leaving her room and coming to him…

Damn. It was too late now to admit he'd made a major mistake when he'd invited her here—into his home, his life.

The next morning Jess cooked breakfast.

'You might be all right,' Michael told her with an unsmiling nod as he made short work of bacon and eggs and hot buttered toast. 'Don't get too fancy, mind you. Just serve up good plain tucker and you won't hear any complaints from me.'

Reece rolled his eyes and Jess suppressed a smile.

'Well, I'm afraid you won't be able to have bacon and eggs every day,' she warned Michael.

'I've given Jess the list of foods your doctor recommends,' added Reece.

Michael scowled. 'Bloody doctors.'

'Oh, I wouldn't worry too much. There are ways and means,' Jess said airily. Already, she was getting used to Michael's grumbles. She could see they were more a habit than genuine gripes and she was actually looking forward to the challenge of winning him around with tasty, healthy offerings.

Once the breakfast dishes were done and Rosie was down for a morning nap, Reece offered to show her the rooms where she and Rosie would sleep. 'I'm afraid they haven't been used for quite a while.'

In fact they were in a part of the house that was locked up and Reece had to wrestle with old-fashioned heavy keys to open a door at the end of the passage that led to them. This done, he hurried forward and opened shutters and windows, letting sunlight stream in to reveal a vast space as well as plenty of dust and cobwebs.

'Hmm…it's worse than I feared,' he said, grimacing.

'But the room's huge.' Jess didn't care about the mess. It would be gone after a day's hard work. More importantly, this bedroom was as large as the entire living area in her previous flat and it had wonderfully high ceilings that made it feel even more luxurious and spacious. Against one wall stood an old-fashioned iron and brass double bed with a mattress swathed in dust sheets, and along another wall stood a matching pair of old-fashioned wardrobes with long oval mirrors on the doors.

Reece pushed open white-shuttered doors. 'And this area needs a thorough clean too, but I thought it might be suitable for Rosie.'

Jess followed him to find a section of veranda that had been closed in with floor-to-ceiling shutters. It was a perfect spot for catching a cooling breeze, or blocking out the sun, and it was also fully fly-screened, which meant she wouldn't have to worry about flies or mosquitoes or nasty creepy-crawlies.

She grinned with delight. 'It's perfect. Actually,

it's better than perfect. It's like something out of my deepest fantasy.'

'And the bathroom's this way,' Reece said, leading the way into an old-fashioned bathroom with black and white tiles on the floor, a separate shower cubicle and a claw-foot bath. Here, sunlight made green and rose window panes glow despite their grime, and there was also a deep cream washbasin set into a marble-topped silky oak dresser.

By now, Jess was practically turning inside out with excitement. 'I can't believe this, Reece. I love it all. Love, love, *love* it.'

She skipped towards him. There was only one thing to do when she was this excited—give the man a great big hug of gratitude. But as she flung out her arms, she heard the sharp intake of his breath, and she stiffened, snatched her hands back just in time.

Yikes. What was I thinking? Reece was her boss and she was a recently bereaved widow. There were boundaries to be kept. Reece had invited her here because he felt sorry for her, not to start something. No wonder he was looking grim and tense, almost angry.

'This is very exciting,' she said instead, and she felt a pang as she wondered what Alan would think if he could see her now. 'When everything's cleaned, these rooms will be gorgeous—like something out of a magazine. I can't wait to get started.' Then she laughed. 'And that's saying something. I'm not usually fond of cleaning.'

'I'll help you.'

'Oh, no, you mustn't.' She wouldn't dream of asking for Reece's help. 'You're far too busy. You have all your cattle to look after.'

His eyes glinted as he sent her a wry smile. 'The cattle can wait for one more day, and the two of us will knock this over in half the time.'

'But you—'

'I'll show you where the vacuum cleaner is,' he said, ignoring her protest. 'And then I'll collect mops and buckets.'

Cleaning walls and windows didn't normally rank high in Reece's favourite activities, but, funnily enough, working with Jess changed his perspective.

He told himself her enthusiasm was catching, and in a way this was true. It was rewarding to work together and to see the honey-gold timber floorboards emerge from beneath layers of grey dust, or to see white walls and window sills looking fresh and cobweb-free.

But it was equally rewarding to look up every so often to catch Jess's smile…or to see the colour of her eyes…the deep green of a tree-shaded creek.

He didn't mind catching her in profile either. Seeing the curving sweep of her dark lashes was a minor miracle…or the soft curving jut of her breasts…or the tempting inches of bare, pale skin that appeared when her T-shirt lifted.

The thing was…he'd sensed an echoing interest from Jess. A certain look, a breathless awareness…small, innocent signals that drove him wild.

Too many times he was tempted to do something about it. To step closer, certain he'd expire if he didn't let her know that he was desperate to touch her…to kiss her.

But such a move would stuff their plans completely.

This was her first full day here. How hard was it to remember he'd offered her a job, not a relationship?

The poor woman was still mourning her husband. How could he have deluded himself into thinking she was interested?

Proximity was his problem. He wasn't used to having a young woman so close at hand, but that would soon be solved once he started mustering.

Grimy and tired, but exultant, Jess stood back to admire the results of their hard work. 'These are lovely rooms.'

'It'll be good to see them being used again.'

'Have they been shut up for a long time?'

'We've had no use for them,' Reece said, answering her question obliquely. 'Too much housework.'

Jess wondered if his mother had lived in these rooms, but she didn't like to ask, knowing from experience that mothers could be complicated, hurtful creatures. But thinking about Reece as a little boy made her heart yearn in a soft, achy way, which was so *not* how she wanted to feel around him.

Especially not after the day she'd just spent, surreptitiously sneaking peeks at his behind and his muscles and his handsome jaw line—and generally suffering from lust meltdown.

She was ashamed of herself. She was here to earn and to save and to do a good job of caring for Reece's home and his father. She would be grateful when he started on his outdoor work—mustering cattle, or mending fences, or whatever it was that cattlemen did.

Unfortunately…once Reece was distracted by outdoor work, Jess's gratitude was short-lived.

He rose early, just before dawn, so Jess, as cook, rose early too, but there wasn't much conversation as Reece downed a hasty breakfast, grabbed a sandwich and an apple for his saddlebag and disappeared on horseback with two blue-speckled cattle dogs trotting behind him.

Jess knew he was joined on the muster by a couple of men from a neighbouring property, who then returned to their place each night, but even with their help Reece didn't get back to the homestead till after sundown, which meant he was gone for more than twelve hours.

And she missed him.

Which was crazy considering that her life now surpassed her wildest dreams. The cooking and the housework tasks were dead easy compared with working in a busy restaurant. Her accommodation was divine and it was still a daily miracle that she didn't have to pay rent. On top of that, she loved being a full-time, stay-at-home mum with Rosie, and her little girl was really happy and thriving, having at last settled into a good routine.

To Jess's surprise, she even liked the outback. Many mornings she hung out the washing to the accompaniment of the smile-inducing sounds of a kookaburra's laughter. From the kitchen she had lovely views across grassy paddocks and gum trees beneath the blue, blue arch of the sky. She could enjoy the sight of kangaroos sleeping in the shade at noon, or creeping out to graze in the lengthening afternoon shadows. She loved to watch flocks of corellas dive and wheel like fluttering autumn leaves.

It was very peaceful and restorative to be surrounded by nature, far away from the stresses and hassles of the coast. Out here, she could finally begin to forgive Alan for being such a fool with their money. And she didn't even mind Michael's grumpiness. They were rubbing along OK.

All in all, she was happy.

Her life really did seem to be taking a turn for the better. She wished she could trust that it would stay that way, but it was hard to trust the universe when you'd been brought up by a mega-wary pessimist. Jess could still hear her mum's warnings loud and clear.

'Don't get too contented, Jess. Life won't let you, you know. Just when you think you're on top, the universe will pull the rug from under you.'

Her mum's series of temporary 'life partners' had certainly proved that gloomy theory. Men had arrived in her mum's life, apparently doting and caring. And all had gone well for six months or so, but things always took a turn for the worse and they left. By the time Jess was twenty or so, she'd realised that her mum never really got to know the men she lived with. She seemed to keep them at an emotional distance, as if she was actually terrified she might fall in love.

Jess had been determined to be different. She wanted to love wholeheartedly. When she met Alan, she was ready to give her *all* to their relationship. Over and over, actually.

Each time Alan had disappointed her, she'd forgiven him and was prepared to start again. But her mother was right. The rug had constantly been pulled from beneath her. And it happened again on the night of the accident.

Even now…when her life seemed to be turning out OK, she had to fight off that inner fear that something would go wrong.

In the fading light of dusk, Reece perched on the top rail of the stockyard fence, entering details of the mob he'd brought in that day. In one pen there were branded cattle he would truck to a fattening block near Rockhampton. In another were cleanskins he'd found in wild scrub in Warringa's outer extremities.

These beasts would need to be vaccinated and ear-tagged, a job Reece would normally leave till morning, but this evening he was contemplating tackling the task now...before darkness fell.

At least it would give him another excuse to stay clear of Jess.

Reece grimaced as he recognised this unattractive new trend in his thinking. He wasn't proud of his avoidance tactics. He knew it made no sense to invite a woman here to the lonely outback and then ensure she was even lonelier by keeping his distance from her.

Problem was, his invitation for Jess to live with him had been fine in theory. And it was dead easy to justify—he'd offered her security and a chance to be with her daughter while she helped care for his father and looked after the homestead.

But, damn it, this beautifully simple plan

was incredibly complicated when he put it into practice.

With a soft curse, Reece swung down from his perch on the rail. By now the sun was slanting low, sending long shadows across the paddocks. A cool breeze made his short collar flap as he pondered his new problem.

Or rather, a new twist to his old problem.

He knew well that it was crazy to imagine a long-term future at Warringa with a girl like Jess. Eventually, she would need to leave. She would want to head back to Cairns where she and Rosie could join a playgroup and interact with other mothers and kids. Jess would want cinemas and parties, girlfriends—all the things women missed when they came out here. She deserved an easier life. She deserved happiness, not hardship.

In other words…there was nothing wrong with his original plan, but they couldn't afford to complicate it with attraction issues. He certainly couldn't let on how badly he was attracted to her.

And the only way he knew to handle this was to stay well out of her way.

* * *

'So what's Reece up to today?' Jess asked Michael over their mid-morning cuppa. It was a question she asked most days, at morning or afternoon tea, or at lunch.

'Same as yesterday.' He rolled his eyes. 'Rounding up cattle, leadin' them into the yards, drafting out the weaners from the mothers, branding, yarding the beasts he plans to sell.'

'I guess he's going to be pretty busy every day, then.'

'Damn busy.' Michael's eyebrows knitted as he watched Jess spooning mashed vegetables into Rosie's mouth. 'She's not too noisy, after all, is she?'

'Does that mean she's not bothering you?'

'Not yet.'

Jess smiled. 'Glad to hear it.'

Everything was fine, actually. Jess had absolutely no reason to feel twinges of disappointment.

Just the same…there were many nights when Reece didn't get back until after she and Michael had already eaten, and she'd had to leave his dinner on a covered plate in the warming oven. She knew it was probably a paranoid thought, but she'd begun to suspect that he was deliberately avoiding her.

The day in the saddle was long and hot and dusty. Reece showered and changed and ate alone in the kitchen, enjoying corned beef with tomato relish and tender vegetables with a delicious white onion sauce. He had to hand it to Jess. She could turn even the simplest dishes into a gourmet meal.

'Enjoying your tucker?'

'Very much,' Reece agreed as his dad shuffled into the kitchen in his pyjamas and slippers.

'She's a good cook.' Michael was squinting without his glasses.

'Yeah. And I take it you and Jess are getting on OK?'

Michael nodded, pulled out a chair and sat slowly, wincing a little as his old bones creaked.

Reece continued eating. He never minded his father's company, but, from years of living with the guy, he sensed that he was about to find himself on the receiving end of a lecture.

Michael leaned forward. 'Are you going to say goodnight to her?'

'To Rosie?'

The old man snorted. 'To Jess.'

This was a shock. The last thing Reece had expected. Then again, his father had periods of vagueness and weirdness these days. 'She's already in bed, Dad.'

'She's in her room, but she likes to read. She's working her way through the books in the lounge room. I'm sure she's not asleep.'

Frowning, Reece speared a carrot with his fork. 'I don't think I'll bother her.'

'She's lonely, Reece.'

A chill slinked through Reece's veins. His thoughts flashed, without his volition, to boyhood memories of his mother. With unnecessary care, he set his knife and fork on his plate. 'What makes you think Jess is lonely?'

'She asks about you all the time. What's Reece doing today? How long does the mustering last?'

He swallowed as his heart began to pump. 'Jess sees me at breakfast. She could ask me those questions.'

'Maybe.' His dad shrugged. 'She doesn't strike me as the timid type, but I reckon you've got her spooked.'

'That's rubbish.'

For long seconds his father stared at him. His once sharp eyes were now cloudy with age and diminishing health but they hadn't lost their inner steel.

Reece sighed. 'All right. I'll talk to her. I'll make sure she's OK.'

Jess slid a bookmark between the pages of her book and set it on the bedside table. The story, set during the Great Depression, was about a lonely guy whose wife had left him. As a result, the man had to care for their little daughter on his own. Life was tough in the cities during the depression and he'd come to the bush, trudging from farm to farm, looking for work and bringing the little girl with him.

It was really well written, funny in places, but also gripping and touching, and for some reason that didn't quite make sense it kept making her think of Reece. Now, the story was probably going to keep her awake when what she needed was something boring that would put her to sleep.

Resigned to at least try to sleep, she reached for the switch on the bedside lamp. On the point of plunging the room into darkness, she heard Reece's footsteps in the hall. Her fingers stilled.

He stopped outside her door and she sat up straighter, her heart suddenly thumping madly. Did he want to speak to her? She wouldn't mind if he came in—if he knocked and just popped his head in to say hello.

Her nightie was practically neck to knee. No worries there. If only she'd left the door ajar so he'd feel more inclined to communicate.

Hell, why was she waiting?

Flinging off the bedclothes, she swung her legs out of the bed. Her feet hit the floor as she heard his footsteps again. Moving away.

Away…

OK. She knew it was silly, but she went to the door anyway, and opened it. Of course, the passage outside was dark and empty.

Ridiculously disappointed, she closed the door and went back to bed, flopped onto the pillows. Stupid tears stung her eyes.

God, I'm a fool.

Rolling over, she snapped off the light. For a minute there, she'd thought that Reece might be lonely or longing for company. But why would he be lonely? He had thousands of cows and his neighbours for company, as well as his father and the men who drove the big road trains that came to take his cattle to the sale yards.

He was a man of the land and no doubt he had women friends he could visit when he wanted female companionship.

Jess, in the meantime, had Michael and Rosie and this homestead, which grew more beautiful every day from all her polishing and cleaning. She was an ungrateful idiot for thinking she needed more.

Well…she was, wasn't she?

* * *

The sun hadn't yet risen when Reece came into the kitchen next morning. Jess was at the stove, stirring pieces of smoky bacon through a pot of baked beans, and she looked up briefly, the merest ghost of a smile tilting her lips. But almost immediately the smile vanished and she quickly dropped her gaze.

'Morning, Reece.' She spoke without looking at him, nodding instead to the teapot on the table. 'I've made the tea.'

'Thanks.'

'These beans are almost ready.'

Normally, he headed for the table. This morning he walked to the stove.

Jess's dark hair was tied up in a loose knot, leaving her pale neck bare.

He forced his gaze from her to the pot on the stove. 'That smells sensational.'

He was referring to the bacon and the beans, although in truth he was even more entranced by the hint of soap or perfume on Jess's skin. She turned to him, her green eyes wide with surprise, her lips parted.

He longed to lean in, to feel the softness of her lips against his, to taste their rosy sweetness. Damn. This was why he stayed away. He was becoming obsessed.

'Is everything OK?' he asked her.

'I think so.' She frowned. 'Why?'

He tried for an offhand shrug. 'Just wanted to make sure you're not getting too bored with life here.'

'Oh, no.' She answered quickly and moved with haste to retrieve two slices from the toaster. 'Rosie's so much more settled,' she said as she buttered the toast. 'I think she adores having me at her beck and call.'

Reece nodded. 'The house is looking amazing. I can't remember the last time the windows were so sparkling. You don't have to go to too much trouble, you know.'

'I don't mind.' She spooned beans onto the toast and handed the laden plate to him. 'You're working very hard, aren't you?'

'Yeah...' He accepted the plate with a brief nod. 'I know I haven't been around much.'

Her eyes narrowed and when she looked up,

her smile was shrewd. 'Has Michael been talking to you?'

'That's a strange question. Of course he talks to me. He's very taken with you, by the way. And I reckon he's happier than he's been in a long time.'

'That's good to know.' Jess reached for the teapot, pouring herself a mugful of hot, strong tea. 'I like your dad.' She added milk to the tea and leaned against a cupboard, sipping, while Reece started his breakfast.

'He's good company.' She looked as if she might have said something more, but then she pressed her lips together as if to stop herself.

Turning to the bench, she reached for the bread packet and said over her shoulder, 'Roast beef and pickle sandwiches OK for your lunch?'

'Yes, thanks.' Reece knew the conversation had been inadequate. At least he'd tried.

Rosie was cutting another tooth and her afternoons were increasingly miserable, but to Jess's surprise Michael found ways to keep her entertained with old-fashioned games with fingers and toes. "Round and round the garden like a teddy bear…" and "This little piggie went to market" were favourites. And the old man was transformed when he smiled and laughed with the baby.

Jess could see that he'd once been as handsome as his son.

'I wonder if you'd mind keeping an eye on Rosie for me while I grab the washing from the line,' she said. Usually, she sat Rosie on the grass with a few pegs to play with, but there were a few clouds rolling in, possibly bringing rain, and she could unpeg the clothes so much faster if she wasn't trying to keep an eye on where the little girl had rolled to or what she was putting in her mouth.

Michael looked delighted. 'We'll be fine here, won't we, Rosie?'

Jess crossed the stretch of grass to the lines strung between two old mango trees. After living in flats that only had dryers or tiny pull-out lines over the bath, she loved the luxury of hanging washing to dry in fresh, clean air and sunshine. And whenever she took them in from the line, the fabrics smelled good enough to bury her nose in.

This simple little pleasure was one of the many things she treasured about her new life. She was humming to herself as she came back to the veranda.

Michael and Rosie were no longer there.

CHAPTER SIX

JESS stifled her instant flare of panic. Michael had gone inside, taking Rosie with him. No big deal.

'Michael?' she called lightly as she went into the house, expecting to see him in his favourite armchair in the lounge room.

The room was empty.

'Michael, are you there?'

When there was still no answer, Jess felt the first stab of hot fear.

'Michael? Rosie?'

She dropped the washing basket and began to hurry through the house, pushing open doors and calling. There was no sign of them anywhere.

Stop panicking. They'll be in the kitchen.

She ran.

They weren't in the kitchen, or the pantry, or the cold room, and a shot of pure terror ripped through Jess. She tried to tell herself she was overreacting. Michael was a responsible adult— a bit vague at times, perhaps, but not foolish. He'd raised Reece on his own, and he was very fond of Rosie. He wouldn't harm her.

Not intentionally.

Oh, God.

After scouring the house from end to end, Jess raced outside again, checked all the verandas, the broom cupboard, the laundry, the outside loo. She stood at the top of the front steps, scanning the endless paddocks for a sign of the man and her baby. *Please, just a glimpse.*

How on earth could an old man have got so far away so quickly?

She cupped her hands to her mouth and yelled, 'Michael!' at the top of her voice.

The only response was the harsh cry of a distant crow.

Now, Jess's mounting panic exploded. All the love she'd ever felt for Rosie rushed through her like a geyser, filling her with fierce longing and dread. From the moment she'd first seen her baby, she'd been smitten, and each day since then Rosie's cute, sweet little personality had blossomed, twining strong, deep-rooted tendrils around Jess's heart.

Her little girl was such a loving, chuckling, gorgeous, perfect thing.

Please, please let her be all right.

Crack!

At the sound of a stockwhip, Jess's heart jolted. Cattlemen used stockwhips—which meant Reece mustn't be too far away.

The thought had barely formed before she was flying down the steps and over the grass. The gate in the fence was too complicated to stop and try to open. She scrambled over it, poised precariously for a moment on the top as it wobbled, and then jumped down and continued racing across the paddock of grazing cattle.

I hope there aren't any bulls in this paddock.

A stockwhip sounded again.

The sound was coming from beyond a stand of gum trees at the far end of the paddock. Jess's heart was pounding as she ran. She couldn't find a gate at the far end, so she dived through the barbed-wire fence, ripping her T-shirt and flinching as sharp barbs pierced her skin. Too bad. She had to find Rosie and she needed Reece to help her.

She staggered on, gasping now, and with a painful stitch in her side, but at last, rounding the clump of trees, she saw a mob of cattle in a cloud of dust. And stockyards. Men on horseback.

'Reece,' she yelled, but of course he couldn't hear her. He was too busy prancing about, steering his horse back and forth, turning it this way and that as he guided the jostling cattle through a narrow opening into the yard.

She waved her arms frantically above her head, praying it was enough to catch his attention— anyone's attention. And then, as she drew closer to the yards she saw a quad bike near the fence line and she recognised Michael's snowy hair and stooped shoulders as he sat astride the bike.

Charging towards him, she finally saw that his arm was around a small pink and white figure on his lap.

'Rosie!'

Jess sobbed, staggering to them on legs so suddenly shaky they could barely support her.

By the time she reached Michael, tears were streaming down her cheeks.

'Da!' Rosie beamed a happy, one-toothed grin at her.

'Oh, baby!' Jess scooped the little girl from Michael's lap and hugged her tight. Still sobbing, she breathed in the sweet baby smell of her just as huge beasts filled the yard, mere inches away on the other side of the wooden fence, pushing and snorting and stirring up dust with their hard, dangerous hooves.

Horrified, Jess backed away, clutching Rosie tightly to her. 'How could you?' she screamed at Michael above the noise.

With a rev of the bike he rode over to her.

'What on earth possessed you to bring a baby out here?' she cried.

He shook his head, bewildered and frowning. 'What's the matter, Jess?'

'What's the *matter*? You took off with my baby

without telling me. You brought her down here where she could have been trampled!' Jess shot another horrified glance to the snuffling, snorting beasts, now metres away, rather than mere centimetres.

'Rubbish,' responded Michael. 'Rosie's all right. I wanted to show her the stockyards.'

'But she's only a *baby*.'

One stamp of those horrible hooves could have crushed her...

'And you didn't *tell* me you were taking her!' Jess was still shaking with anger and fear. 'I had no idea where you'd gone. Didn't you *think*? Didn't you realise I'd be worried sick?'

Hugging Rosie close, she glared at the old man and he glared back at her, but before either of them spoke there was a drumming of hooves close by. Startled, Jess jumped, and saw to her relief that it wasn't a cattle stampede, but Reece on an enormous black horse.

He frowned down at them from a great height as he reined the horse in. 'What's going on?' He scowled at Jess. 'Why have you brought the baby down here?'

'Ask your father,' Jess cried, but even as the words left her lips she felt bad about dobbing the old man in, especially as the creases in Reece's brow deepened as he swung easily, fluidly, down from his horse.

'Dad?'

Michael bristled. 'You used to love the stock-yards when you were little.'

'But Rosie?' Reece was shaking his head. 'What were you thinking?'

'Nothing happened to you, Reece.'

For long seconds, Reece stared at his father, then he sighed and shook his head. His dark, serious eyes rested on Jess. 'Are you OK?' he asked gently.

'Yes, I'm fine.' Her shoulder was stinging a little from the barbed wire, but already she was beginning to calm down.

'I'll walk you back to the homestead.'

'There's no need, thanks. I can manage.'

'No, you're bleeding.' He was looking at her

shoulder and when she craned her neck, she saw a dark red stain on her ripped T-shirt.

'I did that on the barbed wire, but it doesn't hurt too much.'

'You'll need to get disinfectant onto it. I'll help you through the fences,' he said sternly. 'You don't want to scratch Rosie.'

This was true. Jess looked again at the stockyard filling with cattle. There were two men on horseback manning the gate. 'Can you be spared?'

'Sure. The others can manage now.'

A deviant quarter of her brain was actually noting that Reece looked devastatingly sexy in his Akubra and battered jeans. Under other circumstances, she might have loved to linger and watch him at his work.

However, as he tied his horse's reins to a fence post he frowned at Michael. 'You should come back too, Dad.'

'I'll come when I'm good and ready.' Michael still sounded belligerent, but he was looking a bit shamefaced as well.

Watching him, Jess found herself taking fresh

note of his thinning white hair and his rheumy eyes, his five-day-old beard, as white as hoar frost. She saw his gnarled, arthritic hands scarred with sunspots, such a cruel contrast to the peach-smooth, perfect skin of the baby in her arms.

In truth, the old man was almost as helpless as Rosie, and, with his unreliable memory, he was almost as innocent. Already, Jess was beginning to wish she hadn't yelled at him.

'See you back at the homestead, Michael,' she said gently as they left.

The shadows from the grove of trees were already stretching across the paddock as Reece and Jess walked back. A flock of galahs had been feeding on grass seeds and now the birds rose, revealing deep pink breasts as they circled overhead, grey and white wings flapping.

'I'm sorry this happened,' Reece said. 'I'm afraid my father's "senior moments" seem to be increasing.'

'You don't have to apologise. It's actually my fault. I shouldn't have expected Michael to keep an eye on Rosie. After all, you hired me to keep an eye on *him*.'

Reece shrugged. 'It's a bit of a balancing act, isn't it? One minute he's fine, the next he's—'

He didn't finish the sentence. Instead, he nodded to Rosie. 'I haven't seen her for a while. I'm sure she's grown.'

'She's rocking on her hands and knees these days. I'm sure she's almost ready to crawl.'

'Really?'

'You're missing the fun. She's nearly always asleep when you're around.'

'Yeah, well…'

Another unfinished sentence.

At the fence Reece placed a booted foot on the bottom strand of barbed wire and lifted the other strands high, so Jess could easily climb through unscathed, with Rosie in her arms.

'Thanks,' she said. 'Shall I hold it for you now?'

'I'm fine.' He made it look effortless as he held the rough strands down with one hand and vaulted over them.

Rosie laughed at him and cried, 'Da!'

'Da?' Reece shot a questioning glance to Jess.

'Don't worry, she's calling me Da too. It's her first word, though, so it's cause for celebration.'

'I reckon.' Reece grinned at her and his dark eyes flashed, and it was a lovely moment as the three of them walked together towards the homestead. Jess felt far happier and more *connected* than she had in almost seven long months.

Once again, she felt her old yearnings surface, the dream of an ideal marriage and a home that was more than a rented flat. It was a romantic dream she'd cherished throughout her teenage years, but it had lost its sparkle during her marriage and it had finally died with Alan. It was crazy, *crazy* to let it resurface now.

Reece had employed her for her housekeeping skills. Nothing romantic about that. And how could she forget that she had too many debts to clear before she could even contemplate another relationship? She would never go to a new man burdened by the debts from a previous husband.

Perhaps it was just as well they'd reached the gate at the other end of the paddock.

'Thanks for walking me home.' Jess sent Reece a quick smile.

'I'll come up to the homestead with you. I want to check out that cut on your shoulder.'

Jess knew she must have looked surprised— he'd been so distant lately—and she was sure she could manage the cut on her own. But she didn't want to send him away. *No way.*

'That would be great,' she said. 'Thanks.'

They went to the kitchen and Jess put Rosie in her high chair with a baked crust dipped in Vegemite, the baby's favourite snack.

'The first-aid gear's in the pantry,' Reece said, but as he collected cotton wool and antiseptic Jess realised she faced a new dilemma.

'Um… I'll have to take off my T-shirt, won't I?'

There was momentary silence as Reece turned to her, his dark eyes sharp and bright. She could feel her heart picking up pace.

'Turn the chair and sit with your back to me,' he said quietly, and then a playful smile twitched his lips. 'I won't look.'

She knew she shouldn't feel prudish after everything he'd seen on the night Rosie was born. Back then, however, she'd been too distracted by pain to care. Now, ridiculous flames shot under her skin.

But she had to shake off such nonsense. She was here at Warringa as Reece's employee. Nothing more.

Surely that wasn't too hard to remember?

'This is really going to hurt if you try to get the shirt off by yourself,' he said. 'You'll have to let me help you.'

'Um…no. It's OK. I'll…be OK.'

'Jess, there are bits of fabric caught in the cut.'

'Oh.'

She was almost certainly blushing as he lifted the shirt, gently, gently easing the ripped fabric away. Then she sat, as directed, with her back to him and he began to bathe her skin, but, although he was incredibly careful, every time his hands brushed her she felt fire.

'I think you missed your calling.' She tried to make her voice light. 'First you delivered my baby, now you're tending my wounds. You should have been a doctor.'

She couldn't see Reece's reaction and he made no comment as he continued to dab at her cut. It shouldn't have been sexy, but rivers of heat spread all over her. She was imagining him touching her intimately.

She *wanted* him to touch her intimately.

Wanted it so badly.

'Am I hurting you?'

Jess was too breathless to answer and she had to shake her head, and then she realised she was breathing in rather frantic little gasps. No wonder Reece thought he'd hurt her.

'That should be OK now,' he said at last, with a final dab, and she was practically in mourning as he stepped away.

A wicked imp inside her urged her to turn to him, wearing only her bra, to see how he'd react.

Fortunately, her common sense returned just in time and she remembered that Reece was simply being helpful. He was helping her again, as he'd helped her so many times in the past.

Any romance existed only in her head.

She reached for a tea towel from the back of

another chair and held it demurely in front of her
as she stood.

She looked up and met his gaze.

Oh.

Longing shimmered like fire in his lovely dark
eyes—the same longing she was feeling. Longing mixed with agonising uncertainty.

For ages, neither of them spoke.

She had no idea what to say. Her head was
crammed with unhelpful, lustful thoughts.
Thoughts of Reece's lips exploring her... Thoughts
and yearnings so strong she was bursting.

And Reece looked as spellbound as she felt.

Maybe it was time to admit what was happening? Their chemistry was obvious. Screaming to
be voiced.

But this idea had barely formed before Rosie
dropped her baked crust and began to cry.

Gripping the tea towel against her, Jess hurried to pick up the soggy crust. 'There you are,'
she said, quickly handing it back to her sobbing
daughter.

Then she glanced back to Reece. He frowned, looked away and cleared his throat.

The spell was broken.

'I'll get back to the stockyards now.'

He was already heading for the door.

And he was gone before Jess remembered that she hadn't even thanked him.

She felt a little dazed after that, as if she'd stepped off a fast-spinning merry-go-round. But things got back to normal as she turned her attention to mending bridges with Michael. Fortunately, a hearty beef stew followed by baked chocolate pudding seemed to do the trick. Not so fortunately, his fading memory finished the process.

Although Michael surprised Jess a few days later…

'Guess what day it is today?' he asked with a challenging grin at morning tea.

Jess smiled. 'Well, I know it's Thursday.'

'Thursday the sixteenth.'

'Yes. Is that significant?'

'It's Reece's birthday.'

'Really?' Jess remembered her brief exchange with Reece at breakfast this morning. There'd been no hint. They were back to being super cautious around each other.

'I thought maybe you could bake him a cake,' Michael said.

She tried to ignore the sudden flash of excitement, and she concentrated on watching Rosie as she sat unaided on the floor and banged two blocks together.

'I guess I could make a cake,' she said carefully, trying to pretend that she wasn't already in love with the idea of surprising Reece.

'Only if you feel like it.'

'It's no trouble. Does Reece have a favourite kind of cake?'

Michael pulled a face. 'Dunno. I guess everyone likes chocolate cake.'

'I'll see what ingredients we have.'

'Maybe we could have a bit of a party?' The old man's face was lit by a rare smile.

'Well… I guess…' Given the short notice, Jess thought this was going a bit far. She couldn't really imagine herself, an old man and a baby throwing a party.

But Michael looked so hopeful, and who knew how many years he'd be around to celebrate his son's birthday?

'Of course, we can make it a party,' she said quickly. 'Why not?'

There was something different about the house.

When Reece arrived home, dusty and tired as usual, he couldn't quite put his finger on the change. Was it something about the lights?

He took his boots and shirt off in the laundry and padded through to the shower. Under the pleasing hot pressure he rinsed away the day's grime and ran through the tasks he needed to see to tonight. Paperwork, bills... There was a big bill due on the nineteenth and today was the—

Today was the sixteenth of September—*his freaking birthday*—and he hadn't given it a thought. He was thirty-three. Not that it mattered. Birthdays had never mattered at Warringa. Not since—

Abruptly, he snapped off the taps, stepped out of the shower and snagged a towel. In his room he changed into clean jeans and a shirt, and with the shirt hanging open he went down the hallway, noting that the lights were already out beneath Jess's and Rosie's doors. Nothing unusual there, but he was disappointed.

At least he could look forward to finding a delightful meal waiting for him in the warming oven. Jess had produced some pretty amazing dishes, and he fancied he could smell something quite delicious.

But now, as well, that sense of *difference* returned...

Were the lights in the kitchen flickering? The door was ajar. He pushed it.

'Surprise!'

Whack!

Reece staggered backwards, stunned to find the room full of grinning faces. Ryan and Jim, the neighbours he'd been working with all day. Cath and Bill Anderson from Half Moon station. His dad, grinning from ear to ear. Jess, looking sensational in what had to be, hands down, the most attractive little black dress he'd ever seen.

Candles, stuck in bottles or in tin lids, flickered from every bench top. The table was set with a snowy white cloth and decorated with coloured streamers and the best dinnerware and silver.

'Happy Birthday!' everyone shouted, and before he could react they broke into rowdy rendition of the birthday song.

He felt suddenly weak as a kitten, and he wasn't sure if his knees were still working. A rock the size of Uluru filled his throat and the backs of his eyes stung.

The last time this had been sung for him he'd been five years old.

Halfway through singing, Jess's throat felt too tight to go on. She'd been so excited, waiting for this moment. All day her excitement had mounted as she'd worked hard and fast to pull the party together—making phone calls, cooking, cleaning, hunting through the house for everything she needed. Then, there'd been the tension of getting

Rosie to sleep and keeping everyone else quiet when Reece arrived home.

And now—

Now, he looked so shocked and incredulous and downright emotional Jess wanted to cry. No one should be *that* surprised by a birthday party. Surely?

The song came to an end. Everyone cheered and clapped and moved forward to shake Reece's hand or, in Cath Anderson's case, to give him a kiss and a hug.

At least he was grinning now—the grin was a bit shaky and he was looking a little flushed perhaps, but his smile held as he returned backslaps and greetings. He even hugged Michael, which was nice. And then it was Jess's turn.

Reece stepped towards her and she was suddenly super aware of him. His dark hair, damp and sexily rumpled after he'd towelled it dry. His shirt hanging open to reveal the shadow of more dark hair on his chest.

She must have been staring and he must have noticed, for he quickly did up his shirt buttons.

'Happy Birthday, Reece.' She dropped a quick peck on his cheek and she smelled lemon-scented soap on his skin.

His deep brown eyes were a little too shiny. 'Did you do all this?'

'It was Michael's idea.' This time she didn't feel so bad about dobbing in his father.

'But you organised it. You did the legwork.'

'It was fun.'

His gaze travelled over her and his eyes were so appreciative he made her shiver. 'Thanks,' he said softly.

'Can we eat?' chimed in Michael. 'I'm starving.'

It wasn't a late night. Being country folk, everyone had to face early rises in the morning, but the dinner was a lively affair, the conversation convivial. The Andersons had brought wine, which went well with the baked chicken breasts, smashed garlic potatoes and a side dish of broccoli with pine nuts. The rich chocolate layer cake was a hit.

As soon as he'd eaten Michael retired to bed,

and, after coffees, Reece went out onto the veranda to farewell his guests while Jess started rinsing plates and stacking the dishwasher. She was almost finished when she heard the vehicles driving away. She closed the dishwasher, turned it on. With the first soft swish of the water filling the machine, Reece came back into the kitchen.

'That was amazing,' he said quietly.

'I'm glad you enjoyed it.'

'I did. Everyone had a great time. The food was sensational.'

'If I'd had more warning, we could have invited more people.'

'Jess, it was brilliant. The best birthday party I've ever had.'

'Really?' It was hardly a party.

Reece was smiling as he shook his head. 'Believe me. It was a stand out.'

She caught a flash of sadness in his eyes. It was as quick as the flick of a horse's tail, but she knew she hadn't been mistaken. It made her wonder about all the birthdays Reece had spent alone here with Michael and she felt the strongest urge to reach out and hug him.

Just thinking about it, she felt her skin heat again. To cover the moment, she said, 'Would you like another piece of cake?'

He laughed. 'Why not? Will you join me?'

It was deliciously intimate, sitting alone in the candlelight with happy memories of the party warming them as they ate second helpings of the luscious layer cake.

'So, how long is it since you had a party?' Jess couldn't resist asking.

'Twenty-eight years.'

'Really?'

'My last birthday party was when I was five.'

'Oh, my gosh.'

Reece shrugged, sliced a chunk of cake with his fork. 'Dad never managed to produce cakes or parties. Each year he'd put money in my bank account instead. I guess he hoped it would make up for the lack of a present.'

He gave a smiling roll of his eyes, as if he was trying to make light of it. 'I wanted toys, though.'

'Of course you wanted toys.' Jess's heart ached for the lonely boy he'd been. Her own childhood hadn't been too flash with a cash-strapped single mum and the itinerant 'uncles', but at least she'd always had presents on her birthday. Dolls, books, a bike, perfume.

'What about your mum?' Jess *had* to ask. 'Did she remember you?'

'Sure. She used to send me clothes. I'd make Dad take a photo of me. To send back to her.'

'Oh.'

Clothes, not toys. So not what a boy wanted.

Once again Reece smiled, but Jess could feel the pain behind his smile. She was so glad they'd made an effort today and she vowed there and then that she would always make a big fuss of Rosie's birthdays. She wouldn't spoil her little girl, but she definitely wanted her to grow up feeling loved and special and secure.

They put their cake plates and forks in the sink. Went down the silent passage to their rooms.

In the hallway they paused, inches apart, and Jess could feel her blood pumping. Thundering.

She was sure Reece swayed towards her, and once again she could sense the same killing tension in him that was torturing her. Tonight, her emotions were brimming over. If he wanted to kiss her, she was ready.

So ready and waiting.

More than ready, truth be told.

'Goodnight, Jess,' he said gruffly as he pushed his bedroom door open.

'Goodnight, Reece.'

She was talking to the door.

Perhaps it was just as well, Jess decided much later after she'd finally, *finally* cooled down. If Reece had made a move to kiss her, she might have climbed all over him and made a fool of herself. Much better to have retreated back into their corners.

Their caution was sensible. They'd become closer friends this evening without tipping the delicate balance and finding themselves in a complicated relationship. This was good, Jess told herself, although deep down she was torn between needing to know how Reece really felt about her and knowing they shouldn't and mustn't change anything.

Everything had changed tonight.

Reece stood in his room, looking at the familiar furniture he'd known all his life and knowing that he would never be quite the same again.

Jess probably had no idea how much she'd touched him. For her, the party was a small gesture of kindness, but she'd held out a true hand of friendship. He felt unbelievably happy, as if she'd magically erased the decades of disappointment that had blighted this dubious anniversary.

And Jess had done more than simply throw a party tonight. She'd made entertaining at Warringa look miraculously easy. This evening's simple dinner had been so much fun, and Reece found himself wondering why he and his father hadn't made a bigger effort to socialise. The last thing he wanted was to become a surly recluse like his dad.

But perhaps the biggest thing he'd learned tonight was that keeping his distance from Jess was not only crazy. It was impossible.

CHAPTER SEVEN

THINGS changed a little for Jess after the birthday. Reece wasn't in quite such a rush to get away in the mornings. She usually had the radio playing softly in the background and they got into the habit of listening to the six a.m. news and then chatting about it afterwards.

And Reece seemed to make it back earlier in the evenings too. Many nights now, he was home in time for dinner, and a new pattern emerged. Sometimes, they played a game of five hundred with Michael after the meal. Other nights they watched television, which arrived at Warringa via a satellite dish. Or if Michael retired early, Reece and Jess would read for a bit—in the lounge room together, rather than separately in their bedrooms.

Jess genuinely appreciated his company, loved his quiet humour, his surprising wit, his calmness.

Two weeks later, the last of the cattle were branded and included into the herd, or shipped away to fattening blocks further south. The muster on Warringa was over and Reece spent one entire day lazing, shirtless, in a hammock on the back veranda, drinking icy beer, dozing, reading and cheering Rosie, who'd now started crawling and was turning into quite a little show-off.

Reece announced that Jess had earned a day off too, or at least a break from her normal routine.

'Why don't we go out to the gorge tomorrow,' he suggested. 'Take a picnic lunch and swimming gear.'

'I didn't know you had a gorge. That sounds interesting.'

The gorge was quite spectacular, actually. In many ways it was too good to keep hidden. More than once, Reece had considered reducing the cattle herd and starting up a tourist venture. Michael was dead set against it, though.

At least Jess's reaction to the scenery was gratifying. Her jaw dropped next day when they arrived at the head of the gorge and she saw the rocky escarpments falling away beneath her to the deep aqua-green cavern of water below.

'It's beautiful. But I'll have to hang on to Rosie.'

'Don't worry. I can drive you to a safer spot where we can swim.'

'Are there crocodiles?'

'Not where we're going.'

She sent him a wary smile.

'You can trust me, Jess.'

'Of course I can,' she said softly. 'You showed me that on the night I first met you.'

The shining look in her eyes made Reece want to leap high mountains, fight off wild beasts, light protective fires at the door to her cave.

Actually, Reece did light a small fire when they reached the rock pool where he planned to swim. He made billy tea and they drank from tin mugs, sitting on a rocky ledge and dangling their feet in the cool water, and he enjoyed holding Rosie, who seemed super excited about her new surroundings.

After their tea, Jess changed into her swim-suit behind a rock. She knew she shouldn't feel super self-conscious about appearing semi-naked in front of Reece, but she did, of course. At least the costume was a one-piece in figure-slimming, stretch-mark-hiding black. She stripped Rosie down too and carried her to the water.

This would be her baby's first swim.

It helped to concentrate on Rosie, rather than on the tall, broad-shouldered figure nearby. Reece in bathers was a distraction Jess tried to ignore. With little success.

The water was surprisingly cool and at first Rosie squawked with terror, but she soon adapted, and her cries changed to delighted chortles as she splashed madly, thrilled with this new game.

It wasn't long before Reece appeared at Jess's side, all strapping muscles and sleek satin skin, glistening with water. Jess tried not to stare. She really tried.

'You should have a swim,' he said. 'I can hold Rosie for a while.'

'That'd be great. Thanks.'

It wasn't actually possible to hand the baby over without touching him and, of course, the connection sent a live current shooting through her.

So maddening when she was trying extra hard these days to remain immune. But just being with Reece, she felt restless and edgy, as if she'd swallowed fireflies, and there was a permanent, yearning ache low inside her. It was so unhelpful to be constantly attracted to her boss.

As soon as Reece had a safe hold of the wriggling babe, Jess dived quickly away, and she stayed underwater, skimming over the sandy bottom, over the pebbles and reedy clumps to eventually surface, lungs bursting, at the far end of the pool. At a safe distance.

Rolling onto her back, she floated, looking up at the red rocky walls and the cobalt-blue sky. There was an occasional tree growing out of the wall, miraculously rooted, despite the heavy rains and winds that came with the wet season.

It was a typically picturesque outback scene, the sort of postcard-perfect image many people overseas associated with Australia.

Concentrate on the scenery. Forget Reece. You're lucky to be seeing this place.

So much was different about her life now—the

lovely big homestead, the wide open spaces and now this spectacular gorge. She couldn't imagine going back to living in a tiny flat in the city. But that day would come, of course.

For now, she had to make the most of this fabulous opportunity. Not only was she a full-time mum, but her latest bank statements had arrived, and the horrible amounts that she owed were finally beginning to creep a tiny bit downwards.

Everything could be perfect here.

All she had to do now was swim back to the other end of the pool and take no notice of Reece's spectacular muscles.

Which was impossible, of course, but at least she could busy herself with towels, and with getting herself and Rosie dry.

Michael rolled up the bottoms of his trousers and waded in the shallows. They ate their lunch in the dappled sunlight of an overhanging paperbark, and after lunch Michael curled in the shade and had a nap. Reece took off his shirt—Jess prayed for strength—and he made a sling to carry Rosie and then persuaded Jess to join him on a hike.

'The walking will put her to sleep,' he suggested.

And it will wind me into a fever, Jess thought. But she went anyhow, and it was actually very enjoyable to walk along the rocky floor of the gorge, listening to Reece's laid-back drawl as he talked about the first inhabitants of this country, and showed her some wonderful Aboriginal hand-prints on a cave wall.

'I often think I'd like to open this place up and let more visitors in,' he said.

'Tourists?'

He nodded. 'I've fantasised about building ac-commodation with views down the gorge. People could use canoes or dinghies to explore.'

'Would you really want strangers tramping all over your land?'

'Under supervision. It could add a new dimen-sion to life out here.'

It certainly could, and it would counter the lone-liness factor. Jess's head was already running away, imagining exciting possibilities. 'You'd need a decent cook,' she said.

Reece's eyes flashed. 'I would. Do you know one?'

She was sure he didn't expect her to answer this. His shirtless state was causing her enough problems without discussing impossible fantasy futures with him.

She hoped she'd calm down again once they were back at the homestead, once she was busy with dinner and the nightly rituals of Rosie's bath and bedtime. To her dismay, she was still on edge at ten p.m., and she was still thinking far too much about Reece.

She found it impossible to sleep.

Well after ten, Reece was on the veranda, elbows on the railing, staring out at the moon-dappled paddocks too stirred for sleep. It was impossible when every time he closed his eyes he saw Jess in her bathers, saw her slim, shapely figure, her pale arms and legs, her hair, sleek and wet, the lovely curve of her bum, such a tempting handful.

He'd come out here to switch those thoughts off,

but when he heard soft footsteps in the hallway he whirled around, saw a flash of white.

And there she was.

In her nightdress.

Bloody hell.

Ignoring his body's unhelpful reaction, he took a step towards her. 'Is everything OK, Jess?'

'Yes, I'm fine. I couldn't sleep. I was about to tiptoe down to the kitchen to make a cup of tea.'

But now, instead of continuing sensibly on to the kitchen, she came onto the veranda. Her dark hair was loose and flowing about her shoulders and her long nightdress was made from T-shirt material. In the pale moonlight, her skin looked softer than ever. He could see the lush outline of her breasts, their teasing peaks pushing against the fabric.

Desire thundered through him in rolling waves. He'd been going mad all day, ever since the rock pool. He wasn't sure he had the strength to resist Jess now. If she came any closer…

She stepped closer.

She lifted her face, and in the moonlight her lips

were soft and full and the palest pink. 'What are you doing out here?'

'I'm not sleepy either,' he admitted reluctantly.

She looked up with a tiny smile, and with something else. An awareness. A challenge in her lovely green eyes.

A challenge he couldn't resist.

When she opened her mouth to say something more, he dipped his head and silenced her with the briefest touch of his lips.

She stilled momentarily, then sighed softly, sweetly, and swayed against him, almost as if her legs had given way. As he increased the pressure and slipped his arms around her she melted into him, her lips opening to him like a flower to the sun.

He couldn't quite believe he was holding Jess. Holding her and kissing her. At last. He knew this shouldn't be happening, but she was so sexy and soft and womanly, and willing. And he was burning up with need, driven wild by the taste and smell of her and the slow, sensuous dance of their tongues.

He deepened the kiss, binding her tightly against him, his hands cupping her bottom, holding her where he needed her, her heat to his hardness. And he sensed the wildness running loose in her. Pushing them both to the brink. Oh, God…

He wanted her. Wanted to lose himself in her, but he knew he had to stop.

He must stop.

He'd started this, but he had to stop.

Now.

Before they fell over the edge into madness.

He was trembling as he released her. And then, as they stepped apart, as cool air touched where her silky warmth had been, sanity returned with a chilling rush.

He shot a wary glance to Jess. 'I apologise. That wasn't supposed to happen.'

To his surprise she was actually smiling, but when he shook his head her smile faded. Abruptly, she turned from him and leaned on the railing, looking out into the endless stretch of the night. 'You're right,' she said softly.

He almost wished Jess would argue, tell him he was crazy to worry.

Her shoulders were hunched, her face tight. 'So I suppose we should pretend it didn't happen.'

He almost snatched her back into his arms. 'We have to. It's common sense.'

'Yes.'

But he also knew that it wasn't sensible to keep dancing around each other, trying to pretend that they weren't attracted. They were adults, not silly teenagers.

'If we were still in Cairns,' he said gruffly. 'Or—or damn New York—or anywhere but here, it would be different.'

Lifting her chin, Jess frowned at the stretch of dark countryside rendered invisible by the night. He supposed she must have been wondering why being out here changed the rules.

'Out here there's no point in starting anything,' he said, knowing how inadequate that probably sounded.

He was digging a hole for himself. He should

drop this crazy conversation immediately. Walk away. Go to bed.

But he was captured by the sight of her, staring again, out into the night, her hair rippling about her shoulders like dark water.

'So what are you telling me?' she asked. 'That you live like a monk out here?'

He sighed, closed his mind to the memories of his brief, unsatisfactory encounters in recent years.

Now Jess turned to him, and she looked worried. 'I'm sorry. I assumed you wouldn't have kissed me if you had a girlfriend.'

He glared down at his hands, white knuckled as he gripped the railing. 'There's no girlfriend.' But then, he felt compelled to set the record straight. 'I still shouldn't have kissed you, Jess. I should have shown more respect.'

'Respect?' Her eyes widened as she regarded him with a puzzled smile.

'You're a newly bereaved widow.'

Now she blushed as she whirled away from him. Oh, God.

Her face burst into flames. She hadn't given Alan a thought tonight. She wasn't sure how long bereavement usually lasted. It wasn't that she hadn't grieved for him. Of course, she'd been sad about losing her husband. His death was shocking…and she'd felt a terrible loss, but she'd also been worn down by the reality of their marriage.

Alan had left her with so many problems, and with as many bad memories as good ones. It was hard not to feel resentful now, as if she were still being punished.

She felt a need to explain. 'To be honest, I don't feel guilty. My marriage was pretty rocky. Alan and I had problems.'

Reece's face was grim as he took this in. 'I'm sorry to hear that.'

Jess thought he might leave then, but he remained there, by her side, leaning on the railing, looking out across the dark paddocks. She wondered what he was thinking.

For her own part, she couldn't stop thinking about his kiss—the paralysing moment of anticipation, and then the first thrilling touch of his lips to hers, the bliss of being swept into his arms, of being held against him. And then the blaze of longing, the wonderful craziness...

She couldn't hold back a wistful sigh and when she turned to him and met his steady, dark gaze, she refused to look away. But his eyes were so fiercely intent that she eventually had to look down again.

There was an awkward silence and her heart picked up pace. She knew very well that they had no choice but to forget the kiss. Reece was right. If they'd been in the city they might have had a fling, a bit of harmless fun. But it was pretty hard to have a light-hearted, casual affair when you were stranded in an isolated outback homestead.

She wasn't sure what she should do now. Stand here bursting with tension? Say goodnight? Go make that cup of tea?

Still uncertain, she pushed away from the railing, but as she did Reece reached for her hand.

His touch sent a streak of fire scorching through her.

And then his fingers closed around hers, sending a second heatwave flashing over her skin.

The tension was electric, but neither of them spoke. It was as if they didn't want to break the spell with anything as dangerous as words. And then, Reece tugged gently at her hand.

And it was too hard to stay sensible. She was powerless to resist.

Any lingering awkwardness melted. His arms tightened around her, crushing her doubts and questions. She was smiling as he kissed her forehead, melting as his mouth found her cheek, her ear lobe, her chin, then everywhere…

She tilted her head back so he could kiss her throat, and then his lips trailed lower to the neckline of her nightie.

She gasped as his thumbs gently grazed her breasts through the thin fabric.

'Your room?' he whispered.

'Please.'

Of course it was wonderful, and of course they were pleased with themselves. After weeks of suppressing this need, they could at last lie skin to skin, could at last touch and taste to their hearts' content.

Jess's room smelled of cinnamon and vanilla, and they made love on crisp, clean sheets, and she was pleased that she didn't feel the slightest bit awkward or shy. Reece's touch sent a happy charge running through her and everything felt natural and perfectly right.

She loved the giving and the taking, loved the sighing and smiling as they soared together and clung together. Till at last, they plunged from a great height.

Together.

Afterwards.

They lay, limbs loose and relaxed. Sleepy.

'Wow,' Jess said softly.

'Yeah…' Reece drew a deep breath and let it out slowly. 'Wow's the word.'

She smiled broadly in the darkness. 'And thank goodness Rosie didn't wake up.'

It was possibly the wrong thing to say. At the

mention of the baby, Reece hitched up on one elbow. 'I guess it's time I got back to my room.'

She considered asking him to stay. She would love to go to sleep beside him, and to wake beside him. But that was probably asking too much. After all, without actually saying the words, they'd more or less agreed this wasn't the beginning of a real relationship. Whatever it was, it was casual.

As he rolled from her bed Jess closed her eyes. 'Goodnight, Reece.'

Even though she knew it must happen, she didn't want to watch him walk away from her.

The warm pressure of his lips on her forehead was a surprise.

''Night, Jess.'

Such a tiny gesture, but after he'd gone she felt so much better.

In his room, Reece sat on the edge of his bed, staring hard at a faint patch of moonlight on the floorboards, as if somehow it could provide him with answers or reassurance.

I swore that wouldn't happen.

But, surely, no man in his right mind could turn away from a girl as lovely and tempting as Jess.

Just the same, he wouldn't allow himself to be totally blown away by tonight. Yes, he was walking on air, but now it was time to throw out an anchor. Time to get real, to accept that nothing that felt this good could last.

Jess might be utterly bewitching, and tonight with her had been far and away the best sex he'd ever known, but now he had to get their fabulous lovemaking into perspective. Had to remember that Jess wasn't here to stay. She was here primarily to care for his father, and if Michael passed away she'd shoot through.

No question.

Reece was regrettably familiar with this pattern of women leaving, although, in his twenties, he'd been more optimistic about his chances of lasting happiness. Despite the never-forgotten desolation of his mother's desertion, he'd been confident he would be luckier than his dad.

He'd brought girlfriends home to Warringa.

Girls he'd met on city-breaks, or on holidays, girls he'd met at parties, at mates' weddings, at the races...

Picking up girls had been the easy part, and they'd arrived here bright-eyed and eager, claiming to be in love with his 'cowboy' lifestyle. Some had begged to stay on, but their rosy expectations had never been close to reality. Averill had become depressed by the isolation. Rachel couldn't get on with his dad. Gemma had been bored by the lack of a cinema, or girlfriends to chat and gossip with.

Reece had realised then that when he eventually chose a wife, he'd have to find one among the girls who'd been born and bred in the bush. His needs were quite clear. She didn't have to be great-looking, but she had to be comfortable around horses and cattle. She had to cope with hard work and isolation, and she had to have a genuine love of the outback life.

In the meantime...

He had to come to terms with having Jess Cassidy here. In his life, close at hand, day in, day out.

And what an enticing but complicated thought that was.

Jess wasn't a girl he'd met at a party or on a beach holiday. He'd met her here, at Warringa, on a night like no other, the night her husband had died and her baby was born.

A night of incredible emotional connection.

And that was his problem. He cared too much about Jess and her cute baby daughter.

Now it was time to remember that when they left, they would take a sizeable chunk of his heart with them, just as his mother had.

It was a certainty he mustn't lose sight of.

Jess was sure she went to sleep with a smile on her face, still in a happy swoon. She didn't want to overthink this perfect night, so she'd deliberately shut down her thoughts, and she wouldn't let herself ask questions or worry about it. She simply wanted to relax and absorb this new layer that had been added to the happiness that filled her life now.

As she settled into the pillow she felt more

secure and serene than she had in years. Perhaps ever.

It was no surprise that she slept soundly until Rosie woke around four. Softly, she tiptoed to the kitchen, heated a bottle and brought the baby back into bed with her.

Snuggled against a pile of pillows, she made Rosie comfortable, then lay looking at her little girl in the faint creamy light that crept through the slatted blinds at dawn. She rubbed her cheek against her soft silky hair and breathed in the pink and white smell of her.

She remembered last night with Reece, and happiness bubbled through her, again. A shiver-sweet delight that had everything to do with Reece. He'd been so flatteringly passionate and yet considerate too. As a lover, he was her secret fantasy come true.

It was tempting to make comparisons with Alan, but she wouldn't allow that. In fact, she was becoming increasingly aware now, in this new light of day, that she needed to get her head sorted.

Yes, last night was a really big deal for her.

Huge. Unforgettable. But she had to remember it was a fling, not the start of a new relationship. It had been all about chemistry and it had nothing to do with deeper emotions. She was vulnerable because she'd felt overwhelming gratitude to Reece ever since the night he'd found her on the side of the road.

Looking down at Rosie again, seeing her plump cheeks and the bright concentration in her eyes as she drank, Jess remembered the promise she'd made to her daughter back in Cairns on the night Reece had come to dinner. She'd been sure then that she would get on top of their debts and build a future. Without a man.

She had to stick to that plan. Had to do this alone.

She'd had an unforgettable night with a man who stirred her to her very soul, but it shouldn't happen again.

It was more important than ever to remember that now.

CHAPTER EIGHT

'I'VE been checking out your garden,' Jess told Reece at breakfast a few days later.

He looked up, amused. 'What garden?'

'Near the back stairs and beside the laundry.'

'You can hardly call that mess a garden.'

'Well, it has potential. I know it's mostly grass and weeds at the moment, but I started clearing a corner and I found brick edges and the start of a pathway. There's been a garden there in the past and it's all just waiting to be uncovered.'

Jess envied people with gardens, and, after a lifetime in rented flats, she'd been really excited by her discovery. It was like finding buried treasure. 'Is it OK with you if I keep clearing?'

'Sure. Be my guest.' Reece's dark eyes glowed with a mixture of amusement and admiration… and something else. 'I'll help you, if you like.'

She turned back to the stove so he couldn't see how pleased she was. Despite her resolution to keep her distance, there'd been a happy vibe between them ever since the night they'd made love.

They hadn't talked about it. Reece had been as careful as she was to get 'back to normal', but another barrier between them had definitely fallen. They couldn't help smiling at each other now, and they were both mega eager to please.

It was a dangerous kind of limbo, a happy bubble that couldn't hold for ever. At some stage they would have to talk about what had happened. Perhaps they were both scared? Perhaps it meant too much? Felt too dangerous, after all?

Even working in the garden with Reece would be perilously like playing Happy Families, although Jess couldn't deny that his muscle power would be invaluable.

'I'd actually love to grow a few vegetables and herbs for the kitchen,' she said.

'Great idea,' he agreed. 'I should have been doing that years ago, but running the cattle business has taken up most of my time. As you know, we tend to live on tinned and frozen veggies.'

'Well, I'm happy to get it started. Pity there's no plant nursery around here.'

Reece shrugged. 'It's easy enough to order seeds over the Internet, and I'll have to take Dad back to the doctor in Cairns again soon. We can buy plants while we're there.'

'We? Are you planning for me and Rosie to come too?'

'Why not? You'd like a break, wouldn't you?'

Jess grinned at him. It was another thing to look forward to. Each day, her life at Warringa seemed to keep getting better, despite the silent, lingering question—

How long could it last?

She shook that menacing thought away. 'Actually, I'm glad Michael is seeing the doctor again,' she said. 'I do feel he's slowed down a bit lately, don't you?'

'Yeah.' Reece sighed softly. 'But he'll never admit it.'

He stood and took his plate and cutlery to the

sink. 'We may as well start clearing the garden straight after breakfast, before it gets too hot.' He seemed almost as keen on the garden idea as she was.

It was fun—certainly more fun than a potentially boring job like digging up weeds and grass should have been. After Jess had fixed breakfast for Michael, she set a playpen, a picnic rug and toys under a shady jacaranda tree for Rosie. Reece extracted a wheelbarrow, spades, forks and a hoe from an old garden shed, and together they set to work. Reece wielded the hoe on the tough weeds and clumps of kunai grass, while Jess prised out the roots of the couch grass runners that completely covered the path.

It was rewarding to see the growing mountain of rubbish in the wheelbarrow, while a brick-edged garden emerged beside the house, bordered by a surprisingly beautiful, old-fashioned path made from black and white bricks in a herringbone pattern.

'This is going to be gorgeous, Reece.' Jess was already carried away, imagining clumps of basil and rosemary, and then sage and a ground cover of oregano. Oh, and there'd be parsley, as well, and chillies. And cherry tomatoes. 'We can have a pot of mint under the tap.'

She'd once worked in a restaurant that had its own kitchen garden, and it had become a personal fantasy she'd nursed for years. Until now it had been another pipe dream.

Amazing to think it was coming to life all the way out here. When she'd arrived at Warringa, she'd thought she'd come to the middle of nowhere. Now, this house and the land around it were beginning to feel like the centre of *somewhere*. An increasingly fascinating and alluring somewhere.

Jess realised Reece was smiling at her again. 'Have you any idea how your eyes shine when you're excited?'

'Well, maybe they're a bit like yours?' she suggested shyly and, without warning, the air around them was crackling.

Their clothes and hands were grubby, covered in dirt grass stains, but it didn't seem to matter as

Reece closed the space between them and gathered her in. And Jess decided instantly that resistance was futile. She gave herself permission to forget all her questions as he kissed her.

Time stood still. She closed her eyes and his lips worked their magic and the winter sun streamed gently over them.

It was their little bit of heaven until a grouchy *'Harrumph'* from the veranda brought them springing apart.

'What the hell are you two up to?' Michael roared.

To Jess's blushing relief, Reece remained quite calm. Instead of trying to justify their kiss, he sank his hands into his jeans pockets and strolled over to the veranda. 'Hi, Dad.'

She held her breath, waiting for Michael to demand why his son and the housekeeper were madly locking lips.

'What's all this mess?' Michael demanded, with a glare and a sweeping gesture that encompassed their attempts at gardening.

'We're making a vegetable and herb garden.'

'A *what*?'

'A vegetable and herb garden. You know,' Reece said patiently. 'Tomatoes, lettuce, chives—plants we can eat.'

'We don't need to eat plants.'

'Come on, Dad. Don't play games. You know what I'm talking about. Jess wants to grow things for the kitchen. For salads and to use in her cooking.'

Michael continued to scowl. 'This is a cattle station, not a bloody restaurant.' He shot a surprisingly angry glare Jess's way. 'You've been doing something to those hanging baskets near the kitchen too, haven't you?'

'I've been watering them,' she admitted. 'But I haven't wasted tank water, Michael. I've been collecting the grey water from the laundry.' She'd been pleased with her economy and with the lovely green shoots and fronds now sprouting from the ferns' massive, ancient root systems.

'Don't bother,' Michael growled. 'I hate those ferns. They give me the creeps.'

Reece was shaking his head. 'Dad, those hanging baskets have had struggling ferns in them for as long as I can remember. If they gave you the creeps, you could have tossed them out years ago.'

Michael simply growled again and stomped back inside the house. Not a word about their kiss. Perhaps he hadn't noticed?

He was more upset about the garden.

Rosie began to cry then, and Jess went to pick her up. 'You probably need changing, don't you, kitty?'

With the baby in her arms she turned to Reece. 'I might see if she's ready for her nap.'

But he hadn't heard her. He was staring with a puzzled frown at the space where his father had stood.

'Reece?' Jess stepped closer.

He turned and blinked, as if he'd been miles away.

'Is everything OK?'

'Sure.' He sighed. 'I was lost in the past. Trying to remember. I'm pretty sure my mother planted the ferns in those hanging baskets.'

He hardly ever spoke about his mother, the

woman who'd left so many years ago, leaving Michael alone to raise their son.

Jess had no idea what had driven the woman away, and she didn't understand how she could have abandoned her little boy. Just the same, Michael's reaction to the baskets was strange. Why had he kept the plants in a half-dead state? What was he clinging to? Had he never really forgiven his wife? Was he still bitter and angry after twenty-eight years?

These were sobering questions as she went inside. But as she changed Rosie and smoothed lotion onto her soft skin, she realised it was easy enough to wonder about Reece's parents' relationship, but much harder to examine her own behaviour. A few short minutes ago, she'd shared another kiss with Reece in a moment of spontaneous happiness.

Why, when she'd known it was reckless? Why would she risk giving him the wrong idea when she knew she'd eventually have to leave, just as his mother had?

* * *

As Reece had predicted, the afternoon sun hit the back of the house and it was too hot to garden after lunch. While Michael and Rosie had naps, he went off to tinker with a tractor's motor in the machinery shed, and Jess turned her attention to housework.

She was dusting bookshelves in the lounge room when she came across a particularly smart-looking photo album. As she picked it up to wipe the thick red leather binding a photo fluttered to the floor. Stooping to collect it, she saw a picture of a serious little boy with dark hair and handsome dark eyes.

He was standing at the bottom of Warringa's front steps, dressed in smart-looking black trousers, a white shirt and a neat little striped waistcoat.

The boy had to be Reece.

Jess slipped the photo back into the front of the album, but she couldn't help taking a peek and she soon realised that every photo in the album was very alike, with Reece standing on the front steps.

Frowning, she looked a little closer. Reece was incrementally taller and older in each photo, and he was wearing a different outfit each time. The clothes looked brand-new.

These had to be the photos of his birthday outfits. He'd told her that his mother used to send clothes for his birthday, and he would ask his father to take a photograph to send back to her with his thank-you notes.

Jess knew she shouldn't be prying, but she couldn't resist taking a closer look. She could see almost immediately that the clothes weren't very suitable for a boy living in the outback. Reece had spent his days helping his dad in the stockyards or riding horses, but there wasn't one pair of jeans or riding boots.

In one photo a young Reece was wearing a long multicoloured T-shirt over cord-style shorts with long tube socks and sneakers. In another he wore a knitted pullover in a totally impractical lemon and white diamond pattern.

There were other photos of Reece in lime-green Hawaiian-print board shorts, or ridiculously oversized jeans with an equally oversized black rock T-shirt. Perhaps worst of all was the photo of Reece in his teens, wearing a pale grey tracksuit with legs that were too short, so that the elasticated cuffs rode halfway up his calves.

What had his mother been thinking when she sent her son garments that were practically useless?

Jess looked intently at Reece's face in each photo, recognising the gradual maturing of his handsome features. His mouth was always curved into a careful smile, but anyone who knew him well could see the questions in his eyes, as if he wondered if his mother really expected him to wear this stuff.

Her heart ached for the little boy who'd longed for toys, not clothes. Poor Reece.

No doubt he'd also longed for a mother who understood him and really cared about him. And yet he'd dutifully sent these photos back to her, no doubt hoping they'd please her.

With trembling fingers, she touched a photo of Reece in pale beige wide-legged trousers and a brown button-down shirt with palm trees printed across the chest. A city boy might have worn these clothes to church or to the movies or a party, but how often could Reece have worn this outfit? Any of these outfits?

Her face crumpled and a tear splashed the page. More tears followed. Tears for a little boy who'd been left behind. A boy who deserved so much more.

Up to his elbows in motor parts, Reece was wrestling with a tractor's innards when he heard a sound behind him. He turned and blinked as a stooped silhouette appeared in the brightly lit doorway.

'Is that you, Dad?'

Instead of answering, his father shuffled forward. 'I thought I might find you in here.'

'You're supposed to be having a rest.'

'I'll rest in a minute. I wanted to talk to you first.'

'Everything OK?' Reece reached for a rag to wipe the black grease from his hands as his father shambled closer and slowly, stiffly, lowered himself onto an upturned oil drum.

The old man looked tired and grey, hollow-cheeked.

Reece frowned. 'Are you sure you're OK, Dad? Let me take you back inside. We can talk in there.'

'Stop fussing. I want to talk out here.'

'OK. That's cool. What's on your mind?'

'You, Reece. You and Jess.'

He should have known this would crop up. Their kiss in the garden couldn't have gone unnoticed.

His father's eyes glinted. 'This morning wasn't the first time you've kissed her.' It was a statement, not a question.

'That's my business,' Reece said testily.

'Thought as much.'

'You got a problem with it?'

'I just wanted to warn you to be careful this time.'

'Excuse me?'

'Jess is different, Reece.' The old man raised a shaking finger. 'She's right for you, son. She's a keeper.'

A shocked gasp escaped Reece. 'What the hell are you talking about?'

'You know bloody well. You and Jess, of course.'

'Dad, calm down. You've no idea—'

'No. You listen to me. If you play your cards right with this girl, you could be set for life.'

Reece groaned. The last thing he wanted was his father's endorsement of a possible wife or a life partner. He was hoping to remain sensible about his feelings for Jess. He needed to be fine when he finally saw the end of her time here.

The old man was getting carried away. Just because he enjoyed Jess's cooking. 'You know damn well—if I was on the hunt for a wife, I wouldn't be looking for a girl from the city.'

'Jess might be a city girl, but she's different,' his father insisted again. 'She likes it out here. She's not pretending.'

Reece stared at him. For a second, the old man almost made sense. Jess did seem to like it here. She'd heaped praise on the place and he'd never heard a word of complaint from her.

Then again, she was being paid to live here and

he knew she really needed the money, and she was too smart to bite the hand that fed her.

But he didn't want to stir his father. 'Well… thanks for your advice, Dad. I'll bear it in mind.'

'I hope you do, Reece. I'm dead serious.'

Reece stepped closer, touched his father on the shoulder. 'Now that you've sorted my problems, I'm actually worried about you, old fella. I'm glad you'll be seeing Doc Campbell again next week.'

His father gave a grunt of disapproval. 'Bloody doctors.' But when he tried to stand, he swayed dizzily.

Reece was instantly at his side with an arm around him. 'Easy does it. Lean on me.'

'I'm all right.'

'Yeah, sure you are, but let me walk with you back to the house.'

To Reece's surprise and concern, his father acquiesced, clutching his arm all the way to the house, up the steps and then down the passage to his bedroom. He even let Reece help him to remove his boots, and to assist him onto the bed, accepting the assistance without a word of complaint.

As Reece closed the bedroom door he was recalling the strong, tall hero of his youth. He could so clearly remember his father riding a bucking bronco, or leg-roping a steer, carrying an orphaned calf home on his broad shoulders.

Actually, the day the calf came home was emblazoned on Reece's memory. He'd been so excited as his father put the little fellow down on a bed of hay and then took Reece to the kitchen to mix up a bottle of formula.

'Where's the calf's mother?' Reece had asked.

'She's gone, son. Passed away.'

'Like my mother?'

'Near enough. But don't worry, Reece. The calf will be OK. He's got us.'

As a little kid, Reece had been relieved and reassured to see that the calf had turned out fine, growing big and strong and playful, and eventually joining the herd. He supposed he'd identified with it to an extent. He and the calf could both manage without their mothers. He'd certainly believed in his father's knowledge of how things worked in the world.

Now, he thought again about the message Michael had struggled all the way to the machinery shed to deliver.

If you play your cards right with this girl, you could be set for life.

It was an arresting thought and for an instant Reece felt the possibility glow inside him, filling his head and his heart with brilliant hope. But he had to dismiss it.

He'd lost his naïve faith long ago. He knew that when it came to romance and marriage and happily ever after, his old man didn't have a clue.

Their evenings had fallen into a new pattern. After dinner, if they weren't playing cards with Michael, Jess stretched on the sofa and Reece sat in a nearby armchair. Often they were both reading, as they were this evening—or at least, Reece was reading and Jess was trying to concentrate on her novel. But any minute now, they'd probably go to bed. In their separate rooms.

It was a new form of torture, Jess decided. Each night she wrestled with the stupid fantasy that Reece would make a move again—that she would end up in his lap, or he would tumble onto the couch with her.

Tonight it wasn't just physical yearning. She felt quite emotional too. She couldn't stop thinking about Reece's photo album and she longed to take him in her arms, to give him a thousand kisses and hugs to make up for every one of those unsatisfactory birthday gifts.

As she turned another page of her book she realised she hadn't taken in a single word of the last three pages. She set the book aside with a deliberately noisy sigh.

Reece looked up from his cattlemen's journal. 'Had enough?'

'Just about.' But before he could jump to his feet she quickly asked, 'Do you mind if I ask you a personal question?'

He looked mildly amused. 'I guess that depends on the question.'

'I don't think it's *too* probing. I've been wondering what it must have been like for you when your parents split up. You were only little, weren't you?'

'I was five. Why?'

'That's a long time for you and your father to be living out here on your own.'

'We weren't completely on our own the whole time. We had a succession of housekeeper-governesses until I was twelve. And then I was away at boarding school for six years. After that, agricultural college. But since then it's pretty much been the two of us.'

Jess rolled onto her stomach so she could see Reece properly, and for a moment she simply lay there, admiring his dark hair, his dark brown eyes, the strong lines of his face. 'Can you remember your mother?'

'Sure.' His expression grew serious. 'I've seen her a few times since she left.'

'Do you look like her?'

His eyebrows lifted. 'I doubt it. When she was young, she had long red hair. She was quite beautiful, actually.' His mouth tilted in a rueful smile.

'When I was little I thought she was the most beautiful creature on earth. Beautiful, but unhappy.'

'Did you know she was unhappy even then? When you were only five?'

'Wasn't hard to work out. There were plenty of tears. Especially towards the end, after my brother, Tony, was born.'

Jess hadn't known about a brother. 'Tell me to shut up if I'm getting too nosy, but what happened to Tony? Where is he now?'

'Sydney. My mother took him with her.'

And left you behind?

Could this story get any sadder?

'Don't look so worried, Jess. I was fine here.'

'Of course you were.' She hoped she hadn't looked too appalled, and she tried to cover her reaction with another question. 'Have you seen much of Tony?'

'Once or twice at Christmas. I went to his wedding, and to his son's christening.' Reece had been picking at a loose thread on the arm of his chair, but now he looked up and smiled at her. 'Stop looking at me like that.'

'Like what?'

'Like I'm an orphan out of a Charles Dickens novel. I'm OK. I'm cool about everything. You don't really miss what you've never had.'

Jess nodded. 'That's certainly very true.'

Perhaps she agreed a little too wholeheartedly. Reece sent her a rather searching look. 'So how about you? What's your family like? Do you have brothers or sisters?'

She shook her head. 'It was only ever me and my mum. Not all that different from you, I guess—except we lived in towns along the coast. Mackay, Townsville, Cairns.'

'What about your father?'

'I've never met him.'

Now it was Reece's turn to look surprised. 'He took off?'

'I guess he must have. That or Mum chased him away. My mum was vague about the full story, but knowing her, there's a good chance she never told him about me.' Before Reece could ask, she added, 'My mum died two years ago.'

'Jess, I'm so sorry.'

For a moment, he looked as if he wanted to leap out of his chair and take her into his arms, and she certainly wouldn't have minded. But if that *was* his intention, he restrained himself.

A small silence passed before he asked, 'Do you know where your father lives now?'

'In New York, apparently.'

Actually, there was no apparently about it. Jess knew *exactly* where her father was. In recent years, she'd kept tabs on him via the Internet. 'His name's Richard Travere and he's a chef.'

Reece grinned. 'So you inherited his talent for cooking.'

'I guess I must have.' She gave a shrug, as if it were no big deal, but then she felt compelled to confess. 'When I was little, I used to have dreams about him—that he came looking for me—but I can't honestly say that I miss him.'

'At least you'll have photos of Rosie's father to show her.'

'That's true.' Jess grimaced guiltily as she realised how infrequently Alan entered her thoughts these days. But Reece had raised a good point. She must make an album for Rosie with photos of her father, and she should collect and save any other mementos she could find. She knew what it was like to grow up always wondering, and she didn't want those sorts of questions haunting her daughter.

She would leave out the bad bits. Rosie needn't know about the trouble Alan had left behind.

'I'm in the mood for a nightcap,' Reece said out of the blue, and he jumped to his feet, a frown firmly in place. 'Want to join me? There's not a lot of choice, I'm afraid. It's Scotch or Scotch.'

'Oh.' Jess smiled. 'I wouldn't mind a small Scotch.'

He smiled back at her and returned a few moments later, ice cubes clinking in two tumblers, a bottle hooked in one elbow.

To her surprise he came to the sofa. 'Move over.'

A ripple of excitement eddied through her. Sharing Scotch on the sofa was so unlike Reece. Was he letting down his guard again?

Should she be wary?

Hell, no, she decided a second later as he handed her a glass. She wanted to relax and enjoy this close-up view of lamplight on his dark hair and the warm glow in his eyes, not to mention the tempered strength of his body and long, long legs.

By the time she took her first sip of the smooth, fiery liquid, desire was buzzing through her. She was remembering the taste of passion in his kisses, the taut satin of his skin beneath her hands.

Oh, God. She had absolutely no will power. She would be back in his arms in a blink.

CHAPTER NINE

JESS took another, deeper sip of her drink. 'Reece, I hate to ask, but are we ever going to talk about… that night?'

Despite the leap of desire and the warnings clamouring in his head, Reece managed to speak calmly enough. 'I was wondering the same thing. I know it's dangerous ground.'

Jess pursed her lips as she considered this. 'It would only be dangerous if we got too serious.'

'That's a concern, yes.' He couldn't believe how formal he sounded, but discussing this sort of thing was difficult for him. He was a man of action, not semantics.

But while he couldn't allow himself to believe his father's claim that he could have a happy, long-term future with Jess, he knew there were things that needed settling between them.

Right now, she was sitting with her legs curled, keeping her thoughtful gaze fixed on the ice swirling in her glass. She was wearing pale grey trousers and a sleeveless top in a shade of lavender that was perfect for her pale skin and her dark hair. She looked so lovely he was going mad.

'If you're worried about me getting serious, you can relax,' she said. 'I have no intention of getting in deep with any man. Not for ages. I simply can't afford to get serious.'

She looked up then, and her green eyes were clear as glass. 'And to be totally honest, that's not because I'm grieving, Reece. It's a matter of practicality. I have to plan for the future for Rosie and me, and I can't be sidetracked by relationships.'

'Yes…that's understandable…' He swallowed to relieve the awkward tightness in his throat. 'I need to be practical too. I couldn't get serious about a girl from the city.'

'Of course,' Jess said quickly, perhaps a little too quickly. But then she shrugged. 'Something casual could be another matter. With no strings attached—'

Her self-assurance seemed to desert her suddenly and she dropped her gaze to her glass as colour rose high in her cheeks.

Reece drew a very necessary breath. 'Maybe we're on the same page,' he suggested quietly.

Jess was still staring at her glass, but he knew that her eyes had widened. 'Do you think so?'

'If we both want to keep things casual.'

'No strings.'

'Absolutely no strings. No expectations.'

'So no one will get hurt.'

'I'd hate to hurt you, Jess.'

She looked up again, a small smile shimmering. 'Maybe we *are* on the same page, then.'

Almost in unison they downed the last of their drinks, set the glasses aside. Eyed each other.

Smiled.

Reece reached for her hand, smooth and pale and fine-fingered, and held it in his splayed, callused palm. 'Look at that.'

'Vive la différence.'

It became amazingly simple then. A matter of being with the right person in the right moment.

When he leaned in and touched his lips to Jess's, she melted against him and she kissed him back. She tasted faintly of Scotch and she smelled fresh as flowers. As she linked her arms around him he slid his fingers into the dark silk of her hair.

Need met need.

His need and hers. And everything was OK because they had it all planned. No one would end up being hurt. They were OK. And they were so good together.

They kissed with a comfortable kind of urgency, lips and tongues and hands eagerly exploring, removing clothes, rediscovering.

They made love on the couch and then later, after gathering their scattered belongings, they retired to Jess's bedroom where they made love again at a more leisurely pace this time. Lingering. Slow heat building to blissful oblivion.

And Reece thought: *This is how it can be.*

This was how it *should* be. No pressure. No expectations. No guilt. He'd felt many emotions after making love, but never this uncomplicated happiness.

And Jess seemed happy too as she lay beside him, relaxed and easy, her cheek tucked against his shoulder. Their plan was working.

'Just had a thought,' she said sleepily.

'What's that?'

'Is casual sex usually this good?'

'Does it matter?'

'I hope not.'

A spidery fear crept down his spine. 'Are you actually having second thoughts?'

'No, no.' She nestled against him, pressed a kiss to his shoulder. 'I don't have any doubts. Not about this.'

'Have you finished, Michael?' Jess tried not to sound concerned next evening, when Michael pushed his plate away with half his dinner left uneaten.

'I'm not very hungry tonight.'

She'd cooked a lamb stew, which was one of his favourites, and he usually had a good appetite. When she met Reece's gaze across the table, he looked a bit worried, but he answered her silent question with a faint shake of his head.

'How about a little stewed apple and custard, then?' Jess asked as she removed Michael's plate of stew.

He smiled. 'That'd be nice.' He had quite a sweet tooth.

Jess fixed the dessert with her usual efficiency, pleased that she'd made another of his favourites. Over the weeks she'd spent at Warringa she'd become genuinely fond of Reece's dad, despite the occasional difficult moments. She'd never known her own father or either of her grandfathers, so Michael was the first man from an older generation that she'd spent any amount of time with.

He'd told her stories about his boyhood, spent mostly running wild in the bush in the company of young Aboriginal kids. And he'd told her about his days as a young drover when his team had overlanded a thousand head of wild cattle from Far North Queensland to Rockhampton, spending almost six months on the stock routes.

As a young man he'd even had a stint working

on the pampas in Argentina, and Jess had loved hearing about his adventures in a world totally different from anything she'd ever known.

Tonight she was relieved that Michael ate almost all of his dessert. After dinner, Reece carried a cup of tea back to his father's bedroom and settled him comfortably. There was a small television set on his chest of drawers and he liked to sit in bed, propped by a bank of pillows, and watch his favourite TV shows.

Jess was stacking the dishwasher when Reece came back into the kitchen, a line of worry creasing his forehead.

'First thing in the morning, I'm going to ring Doc Campbell's office. I'm going to try to get Dad's appointment brought forward.'

'That might be a good idea.' Jess closed the dishwasher and came to him, touched a hand to his wrist, a gesture of sympathy. She wished she could tell him that Michael would be OK, but they both knew this might not be possible.

'He's always been so strong.' Reece's eyes were extra dark, as if clouded with worry. 'I know he's old and this has to happen, but it's hard to get used to. I haven't seen him this weak since my mother told him she was never coming back.'

'Really?'

Reece glared at a spot on the floor. 'He had a kind of breakdown then. Couldn't get out of bed.'

'Poor man.' Jess frowned. 'But if he didn't get out of bed, I hope there was someone here to look after you.'

Reece shook his head. 'This was before he hired a housekeeper.'

'So how did you cope? Who looked after you?'

'I looked after myself.'

'Reece, you were only five years old.'

It was impossible. Jess couldn't bear to think of it—a little boy alone and a father prostrated by grief.

As much for her own comfort as for his, she slipped her arms around Reece's waist and rested her cheek against his chest. 'How on earth did you manage?'

'Ate whatever I could find. Anything that didn't need cooking. Bread and butter.' He pulled briefly away from her, looked down with a wry smile. 'The butter was so chunky on the bread. I didn't really know how to spread it. But I found apples, oranges, cheese. Ice cream.'

'What about your father?'

'I tried to feed him, but he would only drink water—and not much of that.'

Jess hugged him close, but then she had to step back, needing air. She felt a little dazed and sick at the thought of Michael becoming so completely gutted by his wife's desertion. He must have suffered the worst possible heartbreak.

'What happened in the end?' she asked. 'Did Michael snap out of it?'

'The Pearsons, our neighbours, called in. Actually, I think my memories are based on their story, rather than the true details. They called the Flying Doctor and Mary Pearson cooked up a big pile of meat and potatoes, and then they took me back to their place. I stayed with them while Dad spent some time in Cairns Hospital.'

'Reece, that's terrible. The poor man.' She shivered, feeling chilled as she remembered the pain she'd seen in the eyes of one or two of her mother's cast-off lovers. 'I didn't realise rejection could hit a man so hard.'

She caught a change in Reece's eyes, a momentary bleakness before his gaze steadied again. 'Dad's never talked about it. He's actually tough as nails. I shouldn't have told you. He'd hate it.'

'I'll never repeat a word. I promise.'

Reece nodded. 'Anyway, he got over it, Jess. He had to. He had no alternative.'

Another shiver sluiced through her and she rubbed at her arms. Reece closed the gap between them and pulled her to him. But to her surprise she couldn't relax. She still felt tense, inexpressibly disturbed by his story.

'I'll make coffee,' she said.

His arms tightened around her. 'I want you, not coffee.'

She smiled, relishing his words, and anything might have happened then, if a small wail hadn't come from a distant bedroom.

'That's Rosie.' Jess sighed. 'She's teething again.'

'I'll see to her.'

'No, Reece. You've got enough worries with your father.'

'I don't mind. Honest. You make better coffee than I do. You see to the coffee. I'll check on Rosie.'

He was already on his way.

'The teething gel's on the cupboard in her room,' Jess called after him.

A pink rabbit-shaped night light glowed in the corner of the baby's room. As Reece pushed the door open he could see Rosie gripping the bars of her cot as she tried to stand on wobbly, bowed legs.

'You're stuck, aren't you, mischief? You tried to stand up, and you don't know how to sit down again.'

As he gently lifted her she was already grinning at him and chuckling.

'Hey, this isn't a game. You're supposed to go straight back to sleep.'

Rosie had other ideas. With a gleeful shriek she clutched at his nose and squeezed and tugged.

'Ouch, ouch, ouch,' he joked, eliciting another chuckle from her.

'Dad-da.'

'No, poppet, I'm not your Dad-da.' But even as Reece said this he felt a pang, as if the baby had fired a pygmy dart straight to his heart.

He wasn't sure if he would ever be a father, and tonight that thought seemed to highlight an emptiness inside him that he'd tried his best to ignore. For years.

Rosie made another grab for his nose, and he caught her tiny hand in his and cradled it against his chest. 'Shh,' he whispered. 'Just as soon as I rub this gel on your sore gums, you're going back to sleep.'

He kissed her soft, golden brown hair. 'Shh.'

She smelled amazing. He supposed it was the scents of baby soap and talcum powder, but she smelled so clean and fresh he could practically eat her. And she felt so soft and tiny in his arms as she let him apply the gel, then snuggled into him like a small koala.

Holding her close, he paced the room, rocking her gently as he'd seen Jess do many times, amazed by how much Rosie seemed to love it, how she cuddled into him, utterly trusting.

Man. This feeling was something else. New and totally unexpected. He was gripped by an urge to protect, and by an astonishing surge of fierce, strange possessiveness. How could any parent ever willingly walk away from a cute little person like this?

With the coffee made, Jess came looking for Reece, but as she reached the door to Rosie's room she hesitated.

He was standing in the soft pink glow of the night light, cuddling her daughter, and the baby girl looked so peaceful and tiny in his powerful arms.

Moments earlier, he'd been assisting his frail, ageing father and now here he was with her baby. This same man galloped on horseback at breakneck speed, rounded up thundering great beasts, wrestled wild and angry bullocks and wielded a dangerous branding iron.

It choked Jess up to watch him now, with his

eyes closed, gently rocking her baby daughter and making soft hushing sounds.

Anyone who didn't know him might assume he was Rosie's father. It was so easy to imagine that he actually loved her baby girl…

Perhaps he did?

The thought caused a sharp pang in Jess's throat. Reece had delivered Rosie. His hands were the first hands to touch her and he'd guided her safely into this world. Without Reece, Rosie might have been born on the edge of a track in the mud and the rain and, God knew, it might have ended in tragedy.

As she remembered how wonderful he'd been that night Jess's throat tightened so painfully she had to clasp her hand over her mouth to stop a sob from bursting out. Quickly, she hurried away before Reece caught her spying on him. And blubbing like a fool.

'So you got her back to sleep?' Jess was pleased she was composed by the time Reece came back into the lounge room.

'Yes, Rosie's out to it again, and Dad's asleep too.'

'All's well, then. Here's your coffee.' She handed the mug to Reece as he sat on the sofa. 'I hope it's still hot enough.'

He took a sip. 'Yes, it's fine, thanks.'

Jess drank her coffee, clasping her mug in two hands, as if somehow its warmth would banish the confusion inside her. She wished she could feel happier tonight, wished she could wind back the clock and feel the way she had yesterday evening, when she'd hurled herself into Reece's arms with hardly a care in the world.

It had been so easy then to effortlessly throw up phrases like 'no strings', and to separate her emotions from her lust. Tonight—only twenty-four short hours later—her emotions were un-ravelling. She hoped it was her hormones—her period was on its way—but she suspected it was way more than that.

Last night she'd been focused inwards when she'd convinced herself that her feelings for Reece were solely about physical attraction. Her desire for him had been all that mattered.

Tonight she was seeing the bigger picture—not just Reece's lonely childhood with a heartbroken father. Not just his alienation from his mother, but also his current worries about his dad's failing health. And now, his inescapable connection to her baby daughter.

It was so clear to her now. She'd only been skimming the surface, not really getting to the bottom of who she and Reece were when they were together. There were so many threads to the ties that bound them, and now she was beginning to understand why sleeping with him had always seemed so much *more* than mere sex.

They'd been fooling themselves if they thought they could have a casual, no-strings affair. They'd both witnessed hard evidence from their parents' lives, and they both knew, deep down, that lovers could damage each other, sometimes without thinking, and sometimes irreparably.

'You're very quiet.'

'I know. I'm sorry, Reece. I'm in a weird mood tonight.'

He made no comment, but he reached over and tucked a strand of hair behind her ear and smiled. It was only a small smile of sympathy, but his eyes were so very dark and clear and compelling, and, despite everything that was troubling her tonight, Jess still wanted him. She knew he could sweep aside her uncertainty and melancholy with a single kiss.

And she let him do exactly that.

Jess woke around dawn, pleased to find Reece still in her bed. She snuggled sleepily against his warm, broad back, draping an arm over his hip, tucking her knees behind the backs of his knees. In her lovely bedroom at the end of the house, with Rosie's little room and their own private bathroom attached, she felt cocooned and safe from the real world.

Beyond these walls, people hurt each other through neglect or selfishness or the making of wrong choices.

She wished they could stay there all day.

* * *

Michael was late for breakfast and Reece went to check on him, while Jess sat Rosie in her high chair and fed her rice porridge.

'Cheeky, cheeky girl,' she told her daughter as she scooped blobs of cereal from her chin. 'Stop blowing raspberries.'

Rosie cackled and banged her spoon on the high chair's tray just as Reece came back into the kitchen.

Jess turned and saw that his face was ashen.

'What's happened? What's the matter?'

'It's Dad.' His eyes looked terrible and his throat worked as if he were swallowing sharp stones. 'He's not— I—I can't—'

He couldn't finish the sentence.

A flame of fear engulfed Jess. 'Oh, no, Reece. No.'

He stood, looking utterly bereft. 'He—he's dead, Jess.'

She took a stumbling step towards him, arms ready to hold him, but she was halted by the stark horror in his eyes.

He was already turning away from her. 'I have to ring the ambulance.' He flung this over his shoulder as he hurried out of the room.

It was the most terrible morning, waiting for the ambulance. Reece stayed in his study, pacing the floor, making phone calls, pacing some more. He felt cold and numb and he wanted to stay that way, at least till the ambulance officers arrived and confirmed the worst.

Jess stayed in the kitchen and baked. She needed to keep busy and she was sure there would be visitors, so she baked the simple staples that Michael had loved—a carrot cake, Anzac biscuits, date loaves, an apple tea cake.

She wouldn't let herself think. She couldn't bear to think about poor Michael, so she concentrated on chopping, weighing, stirring, wiping down floury bench tops. She let Rosie have her way with the pots-and-pans cupboard, bashing saucepan lids together, banging on baking tins with a wooden spoon, and the racket was strangely comforting.

Outside, the sun was very hot and bright, which seemed wrong somehow. Surely, it should have been grey and dreary.

CHAPTER TEN

THE dark clouds rolled in on the day of the funeral, and by the time Jess and Reece arrived back at Warringa the heavy tropical rain was bucketing down.

Jess scooted into the house behind Reece, who was carrying Rosie, doubled over to keep the rain off her, and Jess was reminded of the rainy night she met Reece, when her baby was born. Perhaps it was fitting that it would be raining again now. Before too long, she would have to broach the subject of leaving Warringa.

She and Reece hadn't talked much over the past few days. Reece had retreated again, which was understandable. He'd kept super busy making arrangements for the funeral and notifying people of Michael's passing, attending to his regular jobs around the property, as well as taking long rides on horseback, supposedly checking boundaries.

Jess knew he was hurting way more than he let on. He'd been so close to his father, and he was too caring and sensitive not to hurt. She wasn't surprised that he'd covered his pain with tough armour. And she supposed she didn't really have the right to comfort him, although she wished she could.

To keep occupied she'd cleaned the house from top to bottom. There was always the chance Reece's mother might turn up. After all, Michael was her former husband and the father of her sons.

The funeral was held in a little white wooden church in Gidgee Springs, and a surprising number of people packed into the pews and gathered afterwards in the church hall. Reece's mother had *not* been among the mourners, and as Jess had served afternoon tea she'd battled with murderous thoughts towards the woman who'd caused so much pain.

At least Reece's brother was there to honour his father and to support Reece. A slightly younger, citified version of Reece, Tony Weston declined to stay at the homestead, claiming he had an important court case in Sydney to hurry back to. Jess had spied him briefly chatting with Reece, so that was something at least. And there were plenty of other people wanting to offer their condolences, so Reece was surrounded by friends from all over the district and beyond.

But now, so quickly, it was over.

Jess was on the veranda at Warringa, damp and shivering slightly, as she waited for Reece to unlock the front door.

'I guess you'll need to get Rosie fed and bathed,' he said as he handed her over. 'She was very well behaved today, wasn't she?'

'She had a great time being passed around and having so many people making a fuss of her.'

'While her mum slaved in the church hall's kitchen.'

'I didn't mind.'

'I know you didn't mind, Jess. You never seem to mind and you were fantastic, and I'm really, really grateful.'

He came to her and dropped a quick kiss on her lips. His lips were cool from the rain and the kiss was more courteous than sexy, so it should *not* have made her skin burn, but it was the first physical contact between them in days. Now he shrugged out of his suit coat and tossed it over the back of a lounge chair and began to undo his tie.

As usual, Jess couldn't tear her eyes from him. There was something so very masculine and sigh-worthy about the way he stretched his neck as he loosened the tie's knot and then released the top button on his shirt.

He was, of course, oblivious to her small swoon.

'I'm going to shift a mob of cattle out of the bottom paddock near the creek,' he said.

'Now, Reece? But it's pouring.'

He smiled. 'That's why I have to shift them. If it keeps raining like this all night, the creek might come up and flood that paddock.'

'Can it flood so quickly?'

'It wouldn't be the first time.'

* * *

It was completely dark by the time he got back. Jess had bathed and fed Rosie and settled her to sleep to the lullaby sounds of the rain drumming on the iron roof. Tonight it was even louder than on the night Rosie was born.

Then she put a chicken casserole she'd made a couple of days earlier into the oven to reheat, and, while she waited for Reece, she went to her room and opened her wardrobe. She supposed she should start planning the best way to pack up her clothes and all Rosie's things.

She felt sick at the thought. She wasn't sure she had the strength to leave, and she and Reece hadn't talked about it yet, but the depressing fact was, her job here was finished. Reece had only employed her because he'd needed someone to help care for his father.

Now, sadly, there was no valid reason for her to stay. Perhaps, if she hadn't slept with Reece, she might have stayed on as his housekeeper, but they'd complicated things, and he hadn't bothered with a housekeeper before she came. She didn't fancy staying on as some kind of 'kept woman', and she still had her debts hanging over her head. So there was no point in dragging out the inevitable.

Reece arrived in the kitchen, showered and changed, just as Jess was taking the casserole out of the oven.

'That smells sensational. Perfect for a cool, rainy night.'

'It's one of my favourite recipes,' she admitted. 'I'm sure you've had it before.'

He came over and stood close to her. She was conscious of the warmth of him by her shoulder, watching as she lifted the lid, releasing the aromas of chicken and garlic and herbs.

'We had this on that first night in Cairns,' he said. 'Remember?'

'Oh, yes, of course.' It was the night the repossession guys arrived. A night she'd much rather forget, except that Reece's company and their dinner conversation had been so very, very pleasant.

'We fantasised about a holiday in New York,' she said as she ladled food onto plates.

'So we did. Winter in Manhattan.'

Jess didn't return his smile. The fantasy was more alluring than ever now, possibly because she knew with certainty it could never happen. To her dismay, her eyes welled with tears and she was struggling not to cry.

Keeping her face averted, she concentrated fiercely on dishing up their meal, and by the time they were seated she'd managed to resurrect a half-mast smile. 'So how are your cattle?' she asked brightly. 'Are they all safely away from the creek?'

'Yep. I think they should be fine.'

'I still find it hard to believe the creek could come up so quickly.'

'Actually, it's amazing how fast it can happen. It all depends on how much rain has already fallen further to the north.'

'Does the gorge fill up as well?'

'Everything can flood. The roads can be cut.'

'Are you saying that I could be stranded here?'

Reece gave a shrugging smile. 'Why do you think we have such a big pantry and cold room?'

Something in her expression must have alerted him. He put down his knife and fork, his face suddenly wary. 'Are you planning to leave soon?'

Jess's food went down too quickly and she had to swallow again before she could answer. 'I imagine I'll have to go, Reece. You employed me to help keep an eye on Michael.'

'But we both know you've done so much more than that—with the house and—and everything.'

'Well, yes. I've loved working here. In many ways, it's the best job I've ever had. I suppose I could stay on for a week or two.' *If you keep paying me.* Missing so little as a week's wages would cause a dangerous hiccup in her repayments.

'A week or two?'

She didn't like to suggest that she could stay until he was feeling calmer.

'I—I'll need to find another job.'

Reece's jaw tightened. 'Of course.'

She'd never seen such hardness in his face. 'Maybe tonight's not the night to talk about this.'

'Why not?'

His scowl reminded her so much of Michael she wanted to cry. 'Are you angry?'

'Why should I be angry?'

This was going nowhere. Jess knew it was futile to try to discuss how either of them really felt about her leaving. Those issues were emotional and her employment was a business matter. Besides, on the emotional front they'd made promises to each other. No strings. No ties. No expectations.

Her task was clear. She had to convince Reece that she wanted to leave Warringa, even though it would almost destroy her to walk away from him.

Oh, help.

Her fork clattered from her suddenly nerveless fingers as the painful realisation struck home. She *loved* Reece.

She didn't just lust after him. She loved everything about him—who he was, how he behaved, how his mind worked, even where he lived.

Her romance with Alan had been a youthful whirlwind—the whole 'marry in haste and repent at leisure' scenario.

Her relationship with Reece was different in every way. She knew him inside out. She'd lived with him for eight long weeks and she felt intimately connected to him on so many levels. They were linked by all those strings they'd claimed didn't exist.

She loved Reece through and through, but she wasn't in a position to do anything about it.

Reece was frowning at her now. 'I won't try to keep you here, Jess. Not if you want to leave. I know you said that you have to go. You have plans…'

Yes…she had plans to find a new job, and to keep chipping away the debts she'd inherited. She had plans to one day be free of her most pressing problems and to eventually find a nice little cottage with a garden for Rosie to play in, a kindergarten nearby.

'Jess.'

She jumped as Reece's warm hand closed over hers.

'Are you OK?' he asked gently.

Of course she wasn't OK. She was falling apart at the thought of leaving here. Leaving him.

'Hey.' His harshness had melted, and now the hint of a smile warmed his eyes as he rubbed his thumb over the back of her hand.

She stared at his hand covering hers, suntanned and tough, familiar. His thumbnail was slightly frayed and she felt an impulse to kiss it, to feel that jagged edge drag against her lips.

'You know you don't *have* to go.'

This was so hard. She so, *so* wanted to stay. This man and his home were her versions of paradise. She would stay in a heartbeat if he wanted her to, and if she didn't have such a huge mountain of debt.

It killed her that Reece was being gentle and concerned now. She'd found it easier to be strong when he was angry with her.

'You wouldn't have to stay on as my housekeeper,' he said next, and his dark eyes shimmered with all kinds of emotions. 'You could stay here—'

He stopped, and swallowed awkwardly.

What was he trying to say?

'A live-in lover?' Jess suggested, and, despite the longing that coiled tight and hot inside her, she forced her voice to remain cool.

'As my wife.'

His wife? She gasped as the floor seemed to give way beneath her. This was the last thing she'd expected.

It seemed too big to take in.

Too wonderful.

Too perfect.

If only…

If only she were free. If only she weren't buried beneath those debts. Reece would be shocked if he knew how much she still owed. She couldn't possibly ask him to take on her financial burden.

Her mouth twisted out of shape as she tried to find a way to answer him. 'I—I'm so sorry, Reece.'

His chair scraped on the floor as he rose abruptly. 'Of course,' he said tightly. 'Don't worry. I understand.'

But you don't.

He looked terrible and raw and Jess's throat burned with welling tears. She knew Reece would assume she didn't love him or his lifestyle. He couldn't trust any woman to like it out here.

Oh, God. If only she could explain, but how could she tell him about the debts without implying that she needed his help to pay them? The debts were her problem. She'd inherited them from Alan, and she'd inherited a streak of independence from her mother, and there was no way she could drag the financial troubles from her first husband into a brand-new marriage.

Miserably, she watched the tense angle of Reece's shoulders as he stood at the sink, now with his back stiffly to her.

'If we can get across the creek, you'll want to leave first thing in the morning.' He spoke matter-of-factly, without emotion.

So soon?

'I'll drive you to Cairns.'

'No, I wouldn't expect you to do that. I'll get a bus from Gidgee Springs.'

He turned, his face unrecognisably stony and cold. 'If that's what you want.'

Jess found it too painful to look at him and she dropped her gaze to his plate where the chicken and sauces were cooling and beginning to congeal.

To her surprise, he sat down again and picked up his knife and fork as if nothing had happened.

Reece ate without tasting the food, determined to hold himself together. He couldn't believe he'd been so freaking stupid as to ask Jess to marry him.

Where the hell had *that* come from?

He'd had no intention of proposing to her. What was the point? He'd known from the start that she'd never planned to stay here, and he had enough history behind him to know better. He and Jess had even talked about it and they'd set boundaries. Nice, clear, safe boundaries with no sentimentality or emotion.

Yet somehow tonight, in a crazy moment of weakness, he'd fooled himself into thinking that his dad's suggestion was possible, that he and Jess could have a happy future here. And he'd misinterpreted the soft warmth in her eyes.

Sympathy, yes.

Love?

No way.

Certainly not enough love to sustain her at Warringa through the long hot summers, through the isolating wet seasons, through the difficulties of School of the Air and every other challenge the outback flung at its women.

Unfortunately, his pride wouldn't allow him to go storming off like a wounded bull. He forced himself to eat.

Jess had no idea life could feel so bad. She'd suffered loss and disappointment, but nothing had left her feeling as empty as she felt this evening when she went back to her room to start packing.

It took a while, and, when the clothes were packed, she went through the house, picking up small toys, stray baby socks and picture books. Reece was in his bedroom with the door closed and she moved quietly, not wanting to disturb him, not wanting to face him again this evening.

When she'd packed everything except clothes for the morning and her toothbrush, she showered and changed into a nightdress, slipped into bed and turned out the lamp, then she lay, stiff as a board, staring into the darkness.

Remembering…

She remembered Reece here in bed with her. Remembered his lips on her skin, the pleasurable weight of him on top of her, beneath her, the power and excitement.

She thought about Reece with Rosie, so gentle and loving. Recalled his patience with his dad. Her excitement when they'd first cleaned up these lovely rooms. Remembered right back to the night he'd found her on the edge of the road.

Now, she was losing everything. Losing the best person she'd ever known. And now, after she'd recalled every precious detail of her time here with Reece and every wonderful reason why she loved him, she tortured herself by reliving his offer of marriage.

You don't have *to go. You could stay here...as my wife.*

Oh, God. She should have said yes. The impulse to leap up now and run to him was so strong, Jess needed every bit of her strength to stay, curled in a tight ball of pain, while her head waged battle with her heart.

If she stayed here she could be happy. If she stayed nothing would have to change. She could marry a good and gorgeous man and live in his fabulous homestead, sharing his life, making him happy. He deserved happiness.

Oh, it was still so-o-o tempting, so enticing to shove aside all those strong reasons why she mustn't stay.

But she knew they would catch up with her in time. The universe would once again pull the rug from under her. After all, Reece hadn't actually said that he loved her. And she couldn't accept his proposal without telling him about the debts—and he'd be so disillusioned. He'd never believe she was marrying him for love.

No, she had to be strong for his sake, had to save

him from another bitter disappointment, had to walk away now, before they got in too deep, before she broke his heart, just as his mother had.

But what about my heart?

With a moan, Jess buried her face in her pillow and let the hot tears fall.

She slept deeply, totally drained, emotionally and physically, and woke to a grey and miserable morning. Rosie was already awake and playing happily in her cot, innocently unaware that her life was about to abruptly change.

Dressed, Jess went to the kitchen, planning to make breakfast as usual, but she found Reece was already there with a pot of tea and eggs coming to the boil.

'Good morning, Reece.'

'Morning.' No sign of his usual smile. 'Rosie will have a boiled egg, won't she?'

'Yes, thanks.'

It was awful, so stilted, as if they were strangers. Or enemies. Jess set Rosie in her high chair and the baby banged a spoon and chortled, while

Jess concentrated on feeding her with toast sol-
diers dipped in egg.

'I checked the bus timetables,' Reece said.
'There's one leaving for Cairns at ten. If we leave
after breakfast you'll be in Gidgee Springs in
plenty of time.'

'OK. That's good, thanks. I'm packed.'

'Good.'

Jess's throat was so tight she could barely
swallow her tea, let alone toast. She realised she
couldn't even try to eat the egg. Reece made no
comment when she left it untouched.

As soon as Rosie was finished, she made her
excuses.

'If you leave your bags in the hallway, I'll stow
them in the truck,' Reece said.

'Thanks.'

She couldn't bring herself to ask him what he
wanted to do about the high chair and the cot. He
would probably put them in storage and use them
for his own baby one day.

Oh, God. She was fighting tears as she hurried away.

Ten minutes later, she and Rosie emerged from their little suite of rooms for the last time. Reece was waiting on the front veranda and his dark eyes regarded them sternly.

'All set to go?'

No.

Jess nodded, however, and told herself yet again that she mustn't be selfish. She and Rosie were leaving for all the right reasons. She just had to walk down those steps. Get this over.

CHAPTER ELEVEN

RETURNING to Warringa alone was like taking a step back in time for Reece, back to his painful past…

The empty rooms were all too familiar and yet the heartache was worse than anything he'd ever suffered before. Loneliness now was a physical pain, raw and bleeding.

He saddled a horse and took off, riding for hours till he and the horse were exhausted, but when he came home the house was still empty and the pain hadn't eased in the slightest.

It didn't ease over the next few weeks either. He knew Jess and Rosie were gone, but he kept expecting to hear the baby's giggle, to round a corner and encounter the warmth of Jess's smile.

Somehow, some-*crazy*-how, he had to learn to live without them, but all he really wanted was to chase after them, to at least make amends for the hopeless hash he'd made of his marriage proposal.

You could stay here...as my wife...

Bloody hell. Had any man delivered a less romantic proposal?

No wonder Jess turned him down.

He hadn't given himself even *half* a chance. He hadn't told her about the joy she'd brought into his life. He was so unused to talking about love—the word was barely in his vocabulary. He'd more or less assumed Jess could somehow guess that she and her daughter were precious to him.

It was more than possible that he'd made the same mistake as his dad—never letting the woman he loved understand her true worth. And now history was repeating itself.

There was only one good thing—the expectation of loss was so ingrained in Reece that, despite his despair, he could accept Jess's departure as his fate.

Hadn't he known from the night she arrived in his life that this was how it must end?

* * *

It was a long lonely month after Jess left, when the car arrived. The white city sedan was almost completely covered with red dust by the time it pulled up at Warringa's front steps. The driver was paunchy, with thinning hair combed over his bald patch, and he was wheezing and stiff as he climbed out.

He retrieved a bulging laptop bag from the back seat, slammed the door and squinted up at the homestead.

Reece, in his study, dealing with paperwork, had watched the arrival and now he rose slowly, without enthusiasm. He wasn't in the mood for visitors. He was certainly in no mood to be sociable with a stranger from the city. He didn't bother to smile as he went out onto the veranda.

He met the visitor at the top of the front steps. 'G'day.'

'G'day to you, sir.' The fellow's smile was a borderline grimace. 'I'm here to speak to Mrs Jessica Cassidy.'

Reece stiffened. He'd been trying so hard to put

Jess out of his mind, and now everything he'd ever felt for her came back in a painful rush.

'She isn't here,' he said sternly. 'Perhaps I can help you.'

The caller shook his head. 'I need to speak to Mrs Cassidy personally. Will she be back soon?' He frowned at Reece. 'She's a resident here, isn't she?'

Everything about this fellow bothered Reece. Pale and paunchy, he had the air of a guy who spent way too much time perched on a barstool in a smoky pub. 'Sorry, but who are you? What's this about?'

'Ron Harvey from IMP Financial Services.' He flashed a card and Reece's eyes fixed on two words: *Debt Collectors*.

Fine hairs lifted on his skin.

'It's important that I speak to Mrs Cassidy,' the fellow went on, full of brash self-importance. 'If we can't get recovery of her debt, she'll be appearing in court.'

Reece clenched his fists tightly against his thighs to stop himself from grabbing this unpleasant Ron Harvey and shaking him till his nicotine-stained teeth rattled.

'Are you Mrs Cassidy's partner?' Harvey asked.

'I'm not. The name's Reece Weston.' He didn't offer his hand. 'You could say I'm an interested party.'

'Ah.' Harvey's watery grey eyes widened. 'She owes you money too, does she?'

'No, she doesn't. But I'm concerned. This is serious, isn't it? I assume you haven't come all the way out here for a few dollars.'

'Yeah, you're right. The debt is substantial. Obviously, I can't discuss exact amounts with a third party.' Harvey lowered his voice and leaned closer. 'But I can tell you, I don't drive five hundred kilometres for anything under six figures.'

Reece stood stock still, making sure he didn't flinch. But, hell. What was going on with Jess? He'd known she was cash strapped, but she'd never breathed a word of a problem this size.

'Finding her might be difficult,' he said carefully. 'Mrs Cassidy did work here, but she's left.'

The other man's eyes narrowed shrewdly. 'I

hope you're not covering for her, Weston. I need to know where she is quickly, or her problems will only get worse.'

'Look,' Reece snarled, his anger boiling over. 'I can't help you, and I can't help Jess, because I don't know where she is.' He took a step back, dragged in a breath, willing himself to stay calm. He couldn't imagine how Jess could get herself into so much debt. She was a struggling widow, for God's sake. A single mum.

Ron Harvey cleared his throat. 'I must admit this is not one of the better aspects of my job, but you'd be surprised how many women end up inheriting their husbands' financial mistakes.' He shrugged. 'I'll bet odds this'll end up in court, but it's my job to find her and give her one last chance.'

Reece held out his hand. 'Give me your card. I'll see what I can do.'

Six-thirty a.m.

Reece was waiting outside the café on the Cairns Esplanade when the owner arrived, bleary-eyed and yawning and scratching at his chest, as if he'd climbed out of bed a mere thirty seconds ago.

'What's your problem?' He scowled when Reece blocked his way.

'I'm looking for Jess Cassidy. Is she working for you?'

Jess's former boss rolled his eyes. 'I s'pose you're another debt collector. Sorry, mate. Can't help you.'

'I'm not collecting debts. I'm a friend of Jess's, and I need to find her. I want to help her. So tell me. Does she work here?'

'No, she doesn't. Why would I take her back? She raced off out west and left me in the lurch. Thought she was too good for this place.'

Reece bit back the comment he wanted to make. 'Do you know where she is now?'

The guy shrugged. 'Maybe she doesn't want to be found.'

'And maybe she doesn't know these debt collectors are after her. I told you. I'm here to help her.'

Precious seconds ticked by as Reece was subjected to narrow-eyed scrutiny. 'You've been here before, haven't you?'

'I've dined here, yes.'

'You're the guy she took off with.'

No, I'm the guy she rejected. Reece didn't grace this with an answer.

The other man shrugged. 'Guess it's no skin off my nose. But all I know is she's at the Lime Tree three nights a week.'

'And do you know where she lives?'

'Wouldn't have a clue.'

Jess placed the bowls of spicy Asian noodles under the warmer, ready for the waiter, then dashed back to the stove to give the gravy for the lamb racks a quick whisk.

Blowing her hair out of her eyes, she grabbed clean plates and set them on the stainless-steel bench, spun around to get fresh herbs from the fridge and bumped into a solid wall of six-feet-plus male.

'Ouch!'

'Sorry, Jess.'

She gasped. 'Reece!'

Her heart slammed hard against her ribs. How had he snuck in here? This was crazy.

Fabulous too. She couldn't believe how good it was to see him again. But he was taking up far too much space in the normally roomy kitchen. She shot a frantic glance to Brian and Gil, on the far side of the workspace.

Fortunately, they had their backs to her as they concentrated on their tasks. Gil was plating up delicate seafood salads, while Brian was cooking his specialty ricotta gnocchi.

'What are you doing here?' Jess muttered to Reece.

'Finding you.'

Her knees threatened to give way and she grabbed at the bench for support. 'You can't come in here. I'm too busy. We're flat out.'

'OK. I'll wait for you. Tell me where.'

There was a sound to her left. A waiter had arrived to collect the bowls of noodles and he was staring through the hatch at them.

'I'm not sure what time I'll be finished.' She

shoved him towards the door. 'It could be really late. You have to go, Reece.'

'I'll wait. I'll wait all night. Just tell me where to meet you. It's important, Jess.'

She shook head, completely dazzled by his sudden appearance, by his gorgeousness, by his insistence. She wasn't sure she could deal with this. When she finished work she would be dead on her feet.

'The Night Owl Café,' she said as she pushed Reece through the doorway and closed the door in his face.

It was after midnight and Reece was on his third cup of coffee when Jess appeared, looking tired and pale. The tiredness was expected, but it still cut him to see such obvious signs of weariness in her face and in the slowness of her movements as she made her way to him through the maze of mostly empty tables.

Thank God she'd come. He feasted his eyes on her, loving the familiar mix of her pale skin, dark hair and long, slim limbs. 'Would you like something to eat?' he asked her.

'No, thanks. I've eaten.' Slumping into a seat, she pushed her hair out of her eyes.

'A coffee?'

'It might keep me awake. I'll go for a peppermint tea.'

He went to the counter and paid for her order.

'So…?' she asked when he returned. 'Is everything OK?'

Reece took Ron Harvey's card from his pocket and set it on the table in front of her, watched the flare of fear in her eyes. 'I'm afraid you need to contact this guy.'

'How did he find you? Don't tell me he went to Warringa?'

'He did.'

Jess gave a soft groan and closed her eyes, as if this was one problem too many for her.

'I'm here to help, Jess.'

Her eyes flashed open. 'No.'

She might have said more, but her peppermint

tea arrived, and she nodded her thanks and Reece waited patiently while she took a sip.

But he had to ask, 'Why didn't you tell me about this?'

'It's my problem, not yours.'

'But I could have helped you.'

'I didn't want to land my problems on you.'

If he weren't so worried, he might have admired her independence. He could name women who would have chosen a very different option. 'You'll let me help you now, won't you?'

'Reece, I really appreciate that you came all this way. But you can't help me. It's—it's asking too much.'

'You'd rather go to court?'

'Court?' She stared at him in open-mouthed shock.

Reece tapped the card. 'That's what this guy's threatening.'

'Oh, God.'

'Jess, please. At the very least, you're going to need a friend when you have this meeting with Harvey.'

She was pinching nervously at her lower lip. 'Do you have any idea how much I owe?'

'Something in the six-figure range.'

Her eyes widened in surprise, but then she shook her head again. 'See? It's too much. Nobody has that sort of money lying around.'

'Some people do, actually.'

Slow seconds slipped by as she stared at him, his meaning sinking in. 'But even if you have the money, I can't take it from you, Reece. You've already helped me so much. I can't just go on taking and taking.'

'You can pay me back, then. I'm sure we could negotiate friendlier terms than you're saddled with at the moment.'

Jess was still shaking her head, but he knew she was giving this offer serious thought. She was also very close to tears.

She was making her lip quite red from pinching it, and he longed to kiss her, to make her smile. They'd shared so many smiles, so many good times. 'You've got to stop thinking of me as another employer, Jess. Think of me as your friend. We were lovers, for heaven's sake.'

'That's why I hate the idea of you taking on my husband's debts.'

'Listen,' he said, as patiently as he could. 'It's not wise for you to try to handle this on your own. There are all sorts of ways to manage this. But honestly, the loan wouldn't hurt me. We've had some good years with the cattle business. And my father had quite a surprising amount put away. I had no idea he'd made so many shrewd investments over the years.'

She was listening now, drinking her tea and watching him over the rim of her cup, and listening carefully.

'Fate's handed you a raw deal,' Reece went on. 'But Fate has also given *me* a big stake in your life and in Rosie's life. I'll always have an interest in your well-being.'

Tears welled in her eyes, but at least she was no longer protesting.

Reece kept talking. There were other things, painful matters, he needed to set straight. 'I know

I blurted out a proposal at absolutely the wrong time, Jess, but it was for all the right reasons.'

Jess tried to answer, but the only sound that emerged was a tiny bleat.

'I totally understand that you wouldn't want to live out there,' he said. 'So don't let any of that get in the way now. You really should let me help.'

She lifted a shaking hand to her mouth and glistening tears spilled down her cheeks.

Almost simultaneously, they were out of their seats and she was stumbling into his arms.

Jess clung to him, sobbing, her heart breaking for so many reasons. She was so tired and so very stressed, and Reece was every version of wonderful. Actually, he was really just being himself—gorgeous, kind, sexy and generous—and it was killing her.

She wasn't sure how long she took to stop crying. When she lifted her face from Reece's damp shirt, she felt drained and exhausted but a great deal calmer. Looking around them, she saw that the café was completely empty now, which was no doubt a very good thing. Even the guy behind the counter seemed to have disappeared.

'They probably want to close up this place,' she said as she wiped her face on the sleeve of her chef's coat.

'Where are you staying now?'

'Somewhere—' Crumbs, how could she tell him? 'A few streets away. Walking distance.'

'Is Rosie there now?'

'Yes, I pay someone to mind her.'

'Let me drive you.'

She wanted to say no. She was living in a Charity Hostel, and that was information she'd rather not share with Reece, but suddenly she was too tired to argue. 'Thanks, Reece.'

Of course, he was frowning as he pulled up outside. 'What sort of place is this?'

'A hostel. I'm planning to rent a place soon. This is just a stopgap till I've saved enough for a bond on a flat.'

'For heaven's sake, Jess. What about all the money I paid you?' Almost immediately he sighed and answered his own question. 'It all went towards the debts, didn't it?'

She nodded, pushed the door open. 'Thanks for the lift.'

His hand on her arm stopped her, and she remembered they hadn't finalised their plans to meet with the debt collector. She took Ron Harvey's card out of her pocket. 'Is it OK if I ring you about this in the morning?'

Reece was still frowning ahead at the bald concrete building and the bars on the windows. 'I'm sorry. I can't leave you in this place while I trot back to a luxury apartment. Come with me.'

'To your apartment?'

'I'm pretty sure they aren't all booked. I'll ring and check. You can have your own space. Total privacy. Go, get Rosie now and come with me, and at least have a couple of nights of comfort.'

She must have been staring at him as if he'd given her bad news.

'What's the matter?'

'Why are you being so kind? You mustn't, Reece.'

He sighed. 'Just run and get Rosie and whatever you need. Do it for me, please.'

It was the impatience in his voice that sent her hurrying to obey.

The serviced apartments were top-class luxury with a huge expanse of white marble in the foyer, massive urns of tropical flowers, mirrors everywhere.

Reece had made all the necessary arrangements, while Jess was collecting Rosie, and Jess's apartment, with a cot assembled, was ready and waiting as the lift took them silently to the fifteenth floor. The space was fabulous, facing the sea, with a cool breeze blowing in through sliding white, floor-to-ceiling shutters. The rooms smelled faintly of ginger flowers and Jess's aching feet sank into the thick white carpet. The bed was enormous.

And so was the spa bath where she soaked while Reece settled Rosie back to sleep. Luxury with a capital L. What a pity she was too tired to enjoy it.

* * *

'Hey, Jess.'

She jumped as she heard Reece's voice and felt a hand on her shoulder. Water splashed and a wave washed over her breasts. Yikes, she was still in the bath.

Reece loomed above her, tall, dark and heartbreaking.

'Was I asleep?'

'Out like a light.' His eyes were fierce and troubled as he held a thick white towel. 'Do you need a hand?' There was no levity in his voice. He wasn't flirting.

'No, thanks.'

She waited till he'd left the room before she climbed out of the bath, painfully aware of those happy times in their recent past, when Reece had been intimately acquainted with every inch of her naked body.

Now as she went through to the bedroom, wrapped in the towel, she was assaulted by memories of him in her bed. So much pleasure and passion and sweet contentment, and all of it lost.

There was no sign of him now. Rosie was cosily tucked up in her cot in the corner, and Jess was bone weary. Slipping beneath the bedcovers, she gratefully sank once again into sleep.

Bright sunlight streamed through the shutters—and there were voices on Jess's balcony. Reece's deep voice rumbling in a low murmur in response to baby chuckles.

'How long have you two been out there?' Jess called.

Reece appeared at her bedroom doorway with her daughter on his hip, her two hands beating the air with excitement when she saw Jess. 'Good afternoon.'

'Afternoon?' Jess shot up quickly and realised she was still naked. Hastily she grabbed at the sheet as Reece came into the room and sat on the end of the bed, letting Rosie crawl over the mattress to her.

Jess greeted her daughter with laughter and a kiss and a cuddle, but she was soon frowning at Reece again. 'Tell me it's not afternoon.'

'OK. I was exaggerating. It's ten.'

Ten? She'd never slept so late. Not since Rosie was born. 'You haven't been here all night, have you?'

'I slept on the sofa.'

'Really? Why didn't you go back to your apartment?'

'I knew Rosie would wake at some stage and I wanted you to have some uninterrupted sleep.'

'That's incredibly thoughtful, Reece.'

He shrugged. 'I won't be here long. You might as well make the most of it.' His dark eyes rested on her briefly, softening in a way that made her heart ache, but then he flicked his gaze away to the view through the open shutters. 'I've ordered a room-service breakfast for you. And as soon as you're dressed, we'd better ring your debt collector.'

'Are you still planning to go to the meeting with me?'

'Of course. Come on, Rosie.' He scooped the giggling baby up into his arms again. 'We'll let your mum get dressed. She has a big day ahead of her.'

Jess felt terrible as she watched Reece leave. He was being magnificent. Unbelievably kind and generous and thoughtful. From the night she'd met him she'd been in his debt. Now he wanted her to add money to the list of everything she owed him.

How could she possibly allow him to do that?

But—how could she not?

If she didn't accept his help, she could end up in court. She had to think of Rosie. But she also had to remember that as soon as their financial agreement was formalised, she'd be saying good-bye to Reece again.

'I thought that went quite well,' Reece said once they were well clear of Ron Harvey's office.

'He was a bit of a softie, really, wasn't he?'

'Hell, no, Jess. Don't let him fool you.'

'I'm sure he wasn't fooling. I swear he was al-most reaching in his pocket for a handkerchief at one stage. He was incredibly moved by your gen-erosity, Reece.'

She touched Reece's hand, and he came to an abrupt stop. 'I want to thank you, but it seems so inadequate.'

Reece looked as if he was trying to smile, but couldn't quite manage it. He looked away, his throat working overtime. 'Let's not make a big deal about this. It's something I wanted to do.'

Jess found this so hard. Reece was being so stoical. Again. And any minute now she'd start bawling. 'One thing you simply must let me do is cook dinner for you,' she said.

'Actually… I'm not sure that's a good idea.'

'Don't say no. Please, Reece. Now it's my turn to insist.' She forced a brave smile. 'Think of me as your kitchen genie. Name your favourite dish and I'll produce it.'

He smiled at that, white teeth flashing in his suntanned face. 'OK. You've twisted my arm.'

'And your favourite dish is?'

'How about fish and chips?'

'You're joking,' Jess said, but almost straight away she could see that he wasn't. And it made sense, actually. A man who'd eaten so much beef all his life would hunger for something simple but totally coastal, like fish and chips.

'Well, it won't be any old fish and chips,' she promised, and, true to her word, she cooked coral trout in beer batter with the very best crunchy, salty, potato chips, and sides of wilted greens, slices of lemon and tartare sauce. She hoped it was a straightforward, man-pleasing meal.

And this man did seem to be mightily pleased with it.

There was only one problem. Cooking in the kitchen, preparing a meal they would share, and having Rosie nearby, getting under her feet— was all too familiar. It was like being back in the homestead kitchen, as if they'd returned to a time when they were both ridiculously happy.

Throughout the meal, Reece extravagantly complimented Jess's cooking, but she was aware of underlying pain.

His pain and hers.

And the separation that was now looming so close.

She should have listened to Reece when he said

this dinner wasn't a good idea. She could see now that it created a false scenario that was painful for both of them.

They had to pretend they were nothing more than friends. She had to act as if this gorgeous man opposite her hadn't once asked her to marry him, and that she hadn't turned him down for very good reasons. It was so hard to know that he'd misinterpreted those reasons and she hadn't been able to set him straight.

All in all, the night was a terrible ordeal.

By the time they reached after-dinner coffee, Rosie was asleep, but the baby had been a helpful distraction and now Jess could feel the tension between herself and Reece magnifying tenfold.

It was totally understandable that he left early, and Jess knew she shouldn't be miserable as they said goodnight at the doorway to her apartment. She should be walking on air, pumped up with relief and gratitude and big plans for her future.

Not a chance.

'That was a memorable meal,' Reece said politely.

'I'm glad you liked it. As you know, it was an important occasion for me.' *Good grief. That sounded so stiff.*

Her face was almost wooden. 'I'm going to miss you and Rosie.' His voice sounded rough.

'We'll miss you.' A sob threatened as she said this.

Reece turned to leave.

This was it. The final goodbye.

In the hallway now, almost gone, Reece turned back to her. 'Before I go,' he said sternly. 'There's one thing I'd really like to know.' His dark eyes were so direct, they burned her.

'What's that?'

'Did you knock me back because of your debt?'

Jess was suddenly shaking as a month's worth of regrets and useless wishes welled inside her. But when she tried to speak, her throat was too full. She nodded, blinking tears. 'Yes,' she sobbed. 'It was only about the money. Never about you.'

In a heartbeat, Reece was back inside her apartment, closing the door behind him, leaning back against it, staring at her with hope and a hint of happiness shining in his eyes.

'I'm sorry,' Jess managed to say. 'You've ended up with my debt anyway.'

'You think I care?'

She swiped at her tears. 'I felt so bad. I knew you thought I'd left because I didn't like living at Warringa. And that's so wrong. I love it, Reece. I love the house, the paddocks, the people I've met. I didn't even mind your cow—'

He silenced her with a finger against her lips. 'That's all I need to know.'

He kissed her then, and, oh, my God, how wonderful it was. Jess's blood was singing as his lips sealed with hers, as she leaned in to the hard, solid strength of him, and felt at last his arms around her, holding her, binding her close against his thudding heart.

When at last, too soon, he loosened the hug, he reached for her hands instead. 'OK. I'm going to try again, Jess, because I love you. So much.'

He looked suddenly terrified. 'I'm very much hoping you'll marry me.'

To her horror, Jess burst into tears. 'I'm so sorry,' she sobbed, swiping at her eyes with the heels of her hands. 'I'm not unhappy.'

Not surprisingly, Reece still looked uncertain.

'I'm deliriously happy.' Tears and all, she slipped her arms around his neck and kissed him.

'I've missed you so much,' she told him and she kissed him again. Kissed his jaw, his throat, his lips. 'I love you, Reece. And it's been agony not telling you.'

He touched a trembling hand to the side of her face. 'I've missed you so much. Life's not much fun without you and your cute little daughter.'

'I've been so miserable without you.'

This time when they kissed again she could feel the relief and happiness flowing through them both. At last they had reached the emotional honesty they'd both craved. At last they were free to *love*.

They lay in bed, pleasantly tired and aching and sated, the shutters open to the sea breeze and the moonlight.

'Give me your hand,' Jess said, and she placed her hand against Reece's, palm to palm. 'I could marry you just for your hands, you know. I love how big and rough and manly they are.'

He chuckled. 'And I'm crazy about yours. They're so small and pale and girly. How do you keep them smooth like that when you work in a kitchen?'

'Industrial-strength hand cream.'

'It works.'

'I'll bring a gallon of the stuff to Warringa.' Jess pressed kisses to his hand, relishing the luxury of having him close, to kiss and to touch whenever and wherever she wanted. She didn't want to close her eyes in case he disappeared. 'You know one thing that amazes me, Reece?'

'What's that?'

'You're such a kind and generous person even though you've had all kinds of reasons to be bitter and resentful.'

'I could say the same about you.'

She thought about this, about her mum and her serial lovers, about Reece's mother remaining in bitter silence in Sydney. 'I really, really want to be a good mother.'

'You will be, Jess. I know it. Rosie's a lucky girl.'

'Her luck began with you. It's all thanks to you.'

'Hey, enough with the gratitude. I get to keep the two of you. I'm the winner here, OK?'

'OK.' Jess was smiling into the darkness as she snuggled against Reece while he gently sifted strands of her hair.

She was almost drifting off to sleep when he said, 'I have the best idea for our honeymoon.'

'Wow, I hadn't even thought about honeymoons. Where would you like to go?'

'New York.'

'Really?'

'Why not? We've talked about it and I've always wanted to go there. It's one of the most exciting cities in the world and it's good to get a total change from the bush.'

'Would Rosie come too?'

'Of course. We could hire a nanny to help.'

'Reece, that would be amazing. There's so much to do there.'

'I know, and we'll do it all. All the sights, the shows. And while we're there, we could try to find your father.'

Thud. Jess had been thinking about Richard Travere from the moment New York was mentioned, but she hadn't expected Reece to remember.

'I don't know if that's a good idea,' she said. 'He doesn't even know I exist.'

'Well, it's worth a thought. It doesn't seem right to me—a father who doesn't know he has a daughter as fabulous as you are. And you never know, he might be the one grandparent Rosie can grow close to.'

'That's—that's a nice thought.' Amazing, actually.

Reece kissed her ear lobe. 'Sleep on it.'

'I will. Thanks for the thought, Reece. I love you, you know.'

'I know.'

EPILOGUE

THE restaurant was magnificent, an expansive space, with beautiful arched windows and high ceilings, as well as an outside terrace that overlooked a snowy, but bustling, Upper East Side street. Jess decided the place was trendy, cosy and romantic without overdoing it. She was glowing with approval as she and Reece removed their coats and were shown to their table.

Since arriving in New York with Rosie and a nanny, they'd enjoyed all the usual tourist treats. Museums and art galleries, shows on Broadway, sightseeing bus rides and ferry rides. It was all fascinating and exciting. Busy, busy, busy. Cosmopolitan. Energetic.

Wonderful.

New York, New York.

They'd walked the famous avenues and they'd

spent hours and hours exploring Central Park. They'd eaten hotdogs with mustard on a sidewalk, and they'd breakfasted on scrambled eggs and lox in a diner. And they'd shopped till they dropped.

This evening, Jess was wearing the most divine black and silver twenties-flapper-style dress. Reece had insisted on buying it the instant he saw her in it, and, of course, he'd then had to buy a superb Italian suit to match her fine style. Tonight they felt like film stars. This dinner was to be the highlight of their trip.

'You look stunning,' Reece whispered.

'You too.'

Their excitement was fizzing as exquisitely as the French champagne they sipped while they studied the menu. They finally settled on lamb spare ribs and tuna tartare, and when the meals arrived they were mouth-wateringly delicious.

'So you approve?' Reece asked. 'You reckon the chef knows how to throw a meal together?'

Jess smiled archly. 'I'll admit he's not bad.'

They were talking about Richard Travere, of course, the man she believed to be her father, who was both head chef and owner of this fine establishment. They'd discovered during their Internet searches that he usually made an appearance during the evening, and the chance to see him, even from a distance, had been too huge for Jess to resist.

'I won't actually talk to him,' she'd insisted nervously. 'I'll be happy just to see him from the far side of the room.'

They were eating dessert—chocolate semifreddo for Reece and a hazelnut praline for Jess—when the low buzz of conversation in the restaurant dimmed and eyes turned towards the kitchen.

A tall man in chef's whites strolled through the doorway and Jess held her breath. This was the man whose upwardly spiralling career she'd followed from afar. She knew that he'd worked in Brisbane, then Sydney and finally in New York. He was the man she'd wondered about for so long.

Reece reached across the table and his hand on hers was warm and reassuring. Her heart was galloping, but her husband's touch helped to calm her, momentarily.

Richard Travere was impressive with a tanned, longish, slightly arrogant face and steel-grey hair swept back from a high brow. The arrogance disappeared when he smiled, Jess noted, as she watched him pause to chat with diners.

'Looks like he's talking to everyone,' she hissed in a sudden panic.

'That's what we want,' Reece assured her. 'It's better than coming here and missing out on seeing him.'

She took a deep breath and then another. Seemed there were plenty of chef groupies among the diners tonight. Plenty of beaming smiles as people talked to the famous RT.

He was getting closer. In an attempt to look casual, she lifted her spoon, but she was shaking so badly it clattered against her dessert plate and she had to set it down again, quickly, just as the big man greeted them.

'Good evening,' he said smoothly in a broad

Aussie drawl. 'I'm Richard. How's the meal? I hope everything's OK.'

'It's fabulous,' Reece assured him.

'Amazing,' managed Jess.

'Hey, you're Australians.' The chef's eyebrows lifted in obvious delight. 'What part of Oz are you from?'

'North Queensland,' Reece volunteered because Jess's throat was no longer working.

'Nice part of the world. I was there for a time.'

He smiled directly at Jess and she saw that his eyes were the same shade of green as hers. Her heart was almost leaping out of her chest and she was terrified she might cry.

With a supreme effort she forced herself to speak. 'This dessert is truly delicious.' She gestured to the cinnamon gelato, the espresso gelée and the tiny toasted meringue that accompanied her praline. 'All the flavours are so perfectly balanced and complement each other beautifully.'

'Thank you,' he said graciously, clearly pleased. 'Are you a chef?'

'I am, actually.'

He looked at her again, and his smile froze for a split second. He frowned and something stirred in his gaze, but almost immediately his face cleared, and he gave a small, smiling bow and moved on.

Across the table, Reece was grinning at Jess as he reached for her hand again. 'How was that?'

'Scary.'

'You shouldn't be scared. He seems friendly enough.'

'Yes.'

'Are you still determined you won't tell him who you are?'

She nodded. 'It's best like this. I've seen him. That's enough.'

'Are you sure?' Reece's gorgeous face was full of sympathy and understanding. And concern.

Jess knew that look well, and she loved him for caring, but this father business was too iffy. 'I feel better leaving it like this. After all, you have next to no contact with your mother. We have each other and Rosie, and that means everything to me.'

'Well, yes. It means everything to me.'

They shared a smile brimming with all the reasons they loved each other.

'However,' Reece said, looking serious again. 'The big thing I've learnt from you, my sweet Jess, is that it's worth taking emotional risks. I die a thousand deaths every time I remember how I almost lost you. I was almost too scared to try that second proposal.'

'Oh, Reece.' Every time he told her about this, her love for him deepened, widened. Exploded. She blinked away tears before they wrecked her mascara. 'So you really think I should say something?'

'I do.'

'We'd have to get his attention again.'

'Or maybe not,' Reece said, looking over her shoulder.

She turned, stunned to see Richard Travere coming back to their table.

'Excuse me,' he said with an awkward, lopsided smile. 'I know this might sound strange, but I was wondering if you might possibly know someone I used to know in North Queensland.'

* * *

It was the early hours of the next morning when Reece and Jess walked arm in arm down Madison Avenue. They'd had the most amazing evening. Richard had taken them to his private apartment on a floor above the restaurant and the three of them had talked for hours, making up for all the years, all the silences, all the mistakes.

They'd wept and laughed and hugged.

Now, snow was falling lightly. People still lingered on the sidewalks. Yellow taxi cabs streamed past, and steam rose through vents in the middle of the road. True to its reputation, this city had no intention of going to sleep.

And on this exciting, unforgettable night, neither did Reece or Jess. They had a future to plan.

* * * * *

Mills & Boon® Large Print
April 2013

0313 Rom LP

Mills & Boon® Large Print
May 2013

BEHOLDEN TO THE THRONE
Carol Marinelli

THE PETRELLI HEIR
Kim Lawrence

HER LITTLE WHITE LIE
Maisey Yates

HER SHAMEFUL SECRET
Susanna Carr

THE INCORRIGIBLE PLAYBOY
Emma Darcy

NO LONGER FORBIDDEN?
Dani Collins

THE ENIGMATIC GREEK
Catherine George

THE HEIR'S PROPOSAL
Raye Morgan

THE SOLDIER'S SWEETHEART
Soraya Lane

THE BILLIONAIRE'S FAIR LADY
Barbara Wallace

A BRIDE FOR THE MAVERICK MILLIONAIRE
Marion Lennox